Dedalus European Classics
General Editor: Timothy Lane

# BRUGES-LA-MORTE

*GEORGES RODENBACH*

# BRUGES-LA-MORTE

translated by Mike Mitchell

with an introduction by Alan Hollinghurst

and

The Death Throes of Town
translated by Will Stone

Dedalus

Supported using public funding by
**ARTS COUNCIL
ENGLAND**

Published in Great Britain by Dedalus Ltd
24-26, St Judith's Lane, Sawtry, Cambs PE28 5XE
email: info@dedalusbooks.com
www.dedalusbooks.com

ISBN printed book  978 1 912868 06 3
ISBN ebook  978 1 907650 20 8

Dedalus is distributed in the USA & Canada by SCB Distributors
15608 South New Century Drive, Gardena, CA 90248
Email: info@scbdistributors.com  www.scbdistributors.com

Dedalus is distributed in Australia by Peribo Pty Ltd
58, Beaumont Road, Mount Kuring-gai, N. S. W. 2080
Email: info@peribo.com.au

*Publishing History*
First published in France in 1892
First published by Dedalus in 2005
Reprinted in 2007, 2009, 2012, 2019 and 2020

*Introduction to Bruges-La-Morte copyright © Alan Hollinghurst 2005*
*Translation of Bruges-La-Morte copyright © Mike Mitchell 2005*
*Translation & introduction of The Death Throes of Towns copyright © Will Stone 2005*
*Photos of Bruges copyright © Will Stone 2005*

The right of Mike Mitchell & Will Stone to be identified as the translators of this work
has been asserted by them in accordance with the Copyright, Designs and Patents
Act, 1988

Printed and bound in Great Britain by Clays Ltd, Elcograf S.p.A
Typeset by RefineCatch Limited, Bungay, Suffolk

A C. I. P. listing for this book is available on request.

## Alan Hollinghurst

Alan Hollinghurst is a novelist, poet, short story writer and translator. He is the recipient of numerous awards, including the 1989 Somerset Maugham Award, the 1994 James Tait Black Memorial Prize and the 2004 Booker Prize.

He is the author of six novels: *The Swimming-Pool Library*, *The Folding Star*, *The Spell*, *The Line of Beauty*, *The Stranger's Child* and *The Sparsholt Affair*.

## Mike Mitchell

Mike Mitchell has been a freelance literary translator since 1995 and has published over eighty translations from German and French.

His translation of Herbert Rosendorfer's *Letters Back to Ancient China* won the 1998 Schlegel-Tieck Translation Prize after he had been shortlisted in previous years for his translations of *Stephanie* by Herbert Rosendorfer and *The Golem* by Gustav Meyrink. His translations have been shortlisted four times for The Oxford Weidenfeld Translation Prize: *Simplicissimus* by Johann Grimmelshausen in 1999, *The Other Side* by Alfred Kubin in 2000, *The Bells of Bruges* by Georges Rodenbach in 2008 and *The Lairds of Cromarty* by Jean-Pierre Ohl in 2013. His most recent translations include *The Devil's Road* by Jean-Pierre Ohl and *The Continuation of Simplicissimus* by Johann Grimmelshausen.

## Will Stone

Will Stone is a poet, translator and literary journalist. He has published three collections of poetry: *Glaciation*, *Drawing in Ash* and *The Sleepwalker*.

He has a degree in Literary Translation from the University of East Anglia, Norwich, and has produced prose and poetry translations of the works of Stefan Zweig, Emile Verhaeren, Maurice Maeterlinck, Gerard de Nerval, Rainer Maria Rilke and Joseph Roth, among others.

He lives in Suffolk.

# CONTENTS

**Part 1**
Introduction by Alan Hollinghurst to Bruges-la-Morte     11
Prefatory note     21
Bruges-la-Morte     25

**Part 2**
Introduction by Will Stone to The Death Throes of
    Towns     135
The Death Throes of Towns     141
Rodenbach Remembered?     162
A Note on the Photographs     165
Acknowledgements     166

# PART 1

# INTRODUCTION

The Belgian writer Georges Rodenbach (1855–98) is identified above all with the city of Bruges. It emerged early on as a
subject in his poetry, and in his most famous book, the short
novel *Bruges-la-Morte* (1892), a particular idea of the place –
silent, melancholy, lost in time – found its most intense and
influential expression. It led to something of a cult of Bruges
in the Parisian circles that Rodenbach was by then inhabiting.
Bruges became a destination, treasured for its antiquity and
decay, and Rodenbach's novel, illustrated as it was with
numerous photographs of the city's churches, houses and
canals, itself sold very well there, as a souvenir of a particular
aesthetic vision of the place. In the following years other Belgian artists explored the richly desolate atmosphere of the
city, and Fernand Khnopff, in particular, made a number of
mesmerising paintings which combine photographic preci-
sion with a mood of lonely Symbolist contemplation. As it
happened, it was a moment when there was talk of reopening
the city to the modern world after centuries of decline
brought about by the silting-up of its old sea-canal (the new
port of Zeebrugge would be the result). Many Brugeois
resented seeing the epithet *Morte* attached to a city seeking a
new commercial life. Rodenbach would address these
dilemmas, and the possible desecration of his dream-Bruges,
in his last novel *Le Carilloneur* (1897). Was the place to be
loved for its life or for its beautiful death?

Rodenbach, as apologist for the beautiful death, was seen
by Parisians as himself a sort of emanation of the city. In a
memoir written by Paul and Victor Margueritte, who met

11

him at Mallarmé's Tuesday gatherings, he appears as a distinctly 'northern' type, with his light blond hair, pale complexion and 'blue-grey eyes – the mirror of his native skies – those eyes so deep and distant, the colour of the canals that they had long reflected, the colour of still water and moving sky'. In 1895 the French painter Lucien Lévy-Dhurmer produced an extraordinary portrait of Rodenbach, placing him in spectral close-up against a background of the city's roofs and gables, with the great Gothic spire of the church of Notre Dame in wintry silhouette. The writer's grey shoulders seem to rise out of the shadowy waters of the canal behind him. Rodenbach was an elegant, almost dandyish dresser, but Lévy-Dhurmer shows him with his shirt collar undone and with a wide-eyed expression of reverie bordering on grief. Anyone who has read *Bruges-la-Morte* is likely to see this as a kind of double portrait, of the author and of his bereaved and obsessive hero, Hugues Viane, haunting the deserted quays, in strange subjection to his chosen city.

In the little preface which Rodenbach wrote to explain the inclusion of photographs in the book, he describes Hugues's story as 'a study of passion' whose 'other principal aim' is the evocation of a Town, not merely as a backdrop, but as an 'essential character, associated with states of mind, counselling, dissuading, inducing the hero to act'. The photographs are intended to help readers themselves to 'come under the influence of the Town, feel the pervasive presence of the waters from close to, experience for themselves the shadow cast over the text by the tall towers'. This elaboration of mere atmosphere into a principle of action is certainly the central curiosity and mystery of the novel; though it may seem odd that the author should have wanted to supplement his own verbal atmosphere, in all its obscure Symbolist refinement, with the illustrations of a Baedeker.

One needs to look at Rodenbach's own life to understand why the city was able to assume this power of suggestion for him. His connexion with it was aptly both indirect and suggestive. Though Flemish, he was not himself Brugeois. His father was, and it is surely significant for the son's work that he spoke constantly of the place to his children; but Georges was born in Tournai, and grew up in Ghent, also a richly historic city, but one which had adapted itself to the possibilities of modern industry and commerce (Rodenbach *père* was an inspector of weights and measures). Georges was educated at the Jesuit Collège de Sainte-Barbe, as were his exact contemporary and friend Emile Verhaeren, who was to become the leading Flemish poet of the period, and Maurice Maeterlinck, the Flemish writer who was to gain the most international renown, culminating in the Nobel Prize in 1911. (All of them, as members of the educated bourgeoisie, spoke and wrote in French.) Like Verhaeren and Maeterlinck, Rodenbach studied law at the University of Ghent; he then went, in the autumn of 1878, to spend a year as a young barrister in Paris. Once there he immersed himself in a literary culture which seemed to him a luxuriant antithesis to the sterility of Belgium. As he wrote to Verhaeren: 'As for producing literature in Belgium, in my view it is impossible. Our nation is above all positivistic and material. It won't hear a word of poetry . . . Whereas in Paris, one lives at twice the pace, one is in a hothouse, and suddenly the sap rises and thought flowers.' Before returning to Ghent, he published his first collection of poems, characteristically titled *Les Tristesses*.

Back home, he worked for a further ten years in the law but involved himself more and more in the emerging new movement in Belgian literature, as reviewer, essayist and poet. His fourth collection of poems, *La Jeunesse blanche*, published in 1886, was the one in which he himself felt he attained maturity; it is certainly the one in which the mysterious accord between the soul and the city, explored in a mood of lonely withdrawal and silent contemplation, is established: 'To live like an exile, to live seeing no one / In the vast abandonment

13

of a dying town, / Where nothing is heard but the vague rumour / Of a sobbing organ or a chiming belfry' ('Alone', from the sequence 'Soirs de province'.) Silence, he later said, was the thread connecting all his work, his poems being *décors de silence*, his novels *études d'êtres de silence*. The bells that measure out the silence were also to be a recurrent motif, in his poems, in *Bruges-la-Morte*, and of course in *Le Carillonneur*, where the great carillon of Bruges seems to voice the subconscious of the Flemish people.

In 1888 Rodenbach left Belgium for good, and spent the remaining ten years of his life in Paris. Here was the real exile, gladly embraced, and doubly rewarding. He married, wrote, as a kind of two-way interpreter of French and Belgian culture, for both *Le Journal de Bruxelles* and *Le Figaro*, and became a figure – discreet, kindly and punctilious – in Parisian literary life. He was a friend of Mallarmé, whom he revered, of Daudet, the Goncourt brothers, and became close to the proto-Symbolist writer Villiers de l'Isle-Adam, then in the last year of his life. And as his career flowered in Paris, the Flemish subject, the almost mystical nostalgia for Bruges, crystallised for him. The indefinable mood of his poetry, generated from recurrent imagery of empty provincial Sundays, solitude, autumn and winter nightfall, took on a larger fictional form in the light of distance. Rather like A. E. Housman laying claim to an imagined Shropshire while walking on Hampstead Heath, Rodenbach evoked the dead city where he had never lived from his Paris apartment. 'One only truly loves what one no longer has', he wrote. 'Truly to love one's little homeland, it is best to go away, to exile oneself for ever, to surrender oneself to the vast absorption of Paris, and for the homeland to grow so distant it seems to die. [. . .] The essence of art that is at all noble is the DREAM, and this dream dwells only upon what is distant, absent, vanished, unattainable.'

Such a dream dominates Hugues Viane, who finds in the dead city of Bruges a perfect setting in which to grieve for his

14

dead wife. Rodenbach, in his quiet way the most mono-maniac of writers, seems to have found in the unworldly Hugues the persona who could best embody his own obsession. At the opening of the story we see him, a widower of five years, setting out from his big old silent house for one of his solitary walks. Of the house itself we learn little, except that in its drawing-room are the mementoes of his wife, the pictures of her, and the long tress of her yellow-gold hair preserved in a glass case. Hugues, at the age of forty, has made a religion of his sorrow. If in his leisure and sensibility he seems the type of the aesthete, he is a peculiar one, set on the exclusion of all excitement, and on the narrowing of his aesthetic experience to one purpose, the cult of his dead wife. Everywhere he finds analogies to her and to his feelings about her, in the rain, the bells, the canals, until the whole city comes mysteriously to resemble her, to be imbued, as it were, with her absence. He sees intensely but selectively, his eyes being 'fixed on a distant point, a very distant point, beyond life itself'.

This beautiful and refined analysis of grief is the stuff of a Rodenbach poem, but even a short novel needs an element of action, and it is this that is precipitated in the second chapter. Out on his evening walk Hugues turns over thoughts of suicide and of mystical religion, goes into Notre Dame, where he is touched by the imagery of fidelity in the tombs of Charles the Bold and Mary of Burgundy, and then out in the street again sees his dead wife: not the etherealised figure identified with the dead city, but a living woman, apparently her exact likeness. Hugues, himself unwittingly a legend of fidelity in the town, follows her, and then loses her; but we see that an insidious temptation has crossed his path. The pursuit is resumed a week later, when he sees her and follows her again, this time into a theatre, where, conspicuous in mourning, he takes his place in the stalls, unable to see the woman in the audience, and barely aware of what is to be performed.

In fact it is *Robert le Diable*, the extravagantly Romantic opera with which the young Meyerbeer had had his first huge success in 1831, and which had launched the vogue for the supernatural in operas of the mid-century. Balzac was among writers who were interested in it, and in his novel *Gambara* the mad composer of the title gives an analysis of its first performance which must be the most detailed account of a work of music in nineteenth-century literature. But by the 1880s it had fallen out of favour, and it is referred to by Rodenbach as 'one of those old-fashioned operas which almost invariably form the staple of the provincial repertory'. Hugues decides to leave after 'the scene with the nuns', but of course he has left it too late. Rodenbach is shy to exploit the Gothic potential of the situation he has set up, in which the mysterious woman emerges as a dancer, the nun Helena, who rises from her tomb, and seems to the suggestible Hugues to be his lost wife resurrected. Afterwards Hugues recalls the scene as 'a setting full of magic and moonlight', but it is in fact a satanic bacchanal, in which Bertram, a disciple of the Devil, summons up the spirits of those nuns who had died in sin, who shed their habits and work themselves into a frenzy. Escaping from the theatre, Hugues feels himself led on by the vision of the dancer, like 'Faust, reaching out for the mirror in which the divine image of woman is revealed'. The relationship which follows is shadowed from the start by the idea of a diabolic bargain; though who will pay the price, and how, remains uncertain until the final scene.

*Bruges-la-Morte* is a very strange book, by turns both crude and subtle. One remembers it mainly for two things: on the one hand its distillation of mood, its poetic evocation of the impalpable, and on the other its bold, even garish fable of the sexual imagination. The two things are distinct, but not separable, and in a sense highlight the inherent paradox of the Symbolist novel: how is the inwardness, the fatalistic paralysis of Symbolist art to be wedded to the demands of narrative?

Only perhaps in a story that turns on the fulfilment of dreams and a sense of the foreknown. There are of course many currents within Symbolism: the chaste northern reserve of Khnopff's paintings and Rodenbach's poems, with their hinterland of Flemish Catholic piety, coexists with a pre-occupation, even in other Belgian artists, with pagan icons of female sexual power; and it is this tradition of morbid eroti-cism that Rodenbach, perhaps going a little against his natural grain, invokes in the figure of the dancer Jane Scott.

Some contemporary reviewers criticised what they saw as a vein of vulgar sensuality in Rodenbach's treatment of the affair between Hugues and Jane, which emerges as in essence that between a prostitute and an infatuated punter. But Rodenbach is characteristically discreet about the details of what passes between them. Chapter Twelve of the novel offers a convincing analysis of Hugues's powerless descent into lust-ful obsession when the dream of the returned wife is revealed unambiguously as theatre, an effect of make-up and hair-dye; but it is all summary: we are not allowed to witness any of those scenes between them that a more sensational kind of novel might have dwelt on. Similarly, Hugues's married life is recalled at the outset as one of unabating happiness, explor-ation and sexual fulfilment, but nothing concrete is ever said about what the couple did together, where they lived, or even what his wife was called. A deep privacy veils the very object of his devotions, which we are allowed to see only in symbolic form, in the proliferation of analogies.

*Bruges-la-Morte* was also criticised for the improbability of its subject, but a novel of this kind is not to be judged by its likeness to life, or indeed to most other novels. It creates a rarefied world, internalised and intensified by feeling. The conventions of realistic fiction are almost completely aban-doned; the details of the modern life of the city – it has a theatre, shops, markets, gossips and scandals – seem to impinge on Hugues's dream world as if from another kind of novel

altogether. A vague comedy is admitted in those moments
when the town comments illusionlessly on his infatuation.
There is grotesque humour as well as poignancy in the scene
where Hugues persuades Jane to put on his dead wife's
dresses, and is mocked by her for their out-of-dateness. But
the normative irony of the bourgeois novel would be death to
Rodenbach's fable. *Un être de silence* has no society.

At times *Bruges-la-Morte* seems to align itself with a vein of
modern pscychological fantasy, as a study in obsession and
self-delusion, and like Henry James's 'The Turn of the
Screw' admits of an alternative reading, in which the uncanny
similarity of Jane to the dead wife is not offered as a fact but as
a fatal delusion of Hugues himself, a projection of a psycho-
sexual need. No one else in the book knew the dead wife, so
the analogy is tested only by Hugues and at the very end
by Jane herself, who seeing a picture of the wife says that
she 'looks like me', but gives no sign of understanding the
scenario in which she has long been playing a part. Since most
of the novel is experienced through Hugues, we receive a
gathering impression of the viciousness of Jane, as a first passive and then vindictive *femme fatale*; but it is also possible to
see her as the frustrated victim of a man's deranged fantasy.
Rodenbach, it must be said, lacks James's flawless cleverness,
but an element of irresolvable ambiguity is certainly part of
his book's continuing interest.

Above all, though, *Bruges-la-Morte* is the novel of a poet,
who works in rhythm and pattern, image and suggestion. At
its heart lies the essence of poetry: a simile. It is a book about
resemblance, the strange identity of the known and the
unknown, 'the horizon where habit and novelty meet'. The
central resemblance, between one woman and another, is
discovered by a man whose whole world is given value by
resemblances, 'mysterious equations' of past and present,
place and feeling, the seen and the unknowable. The prose
in which Rodenbach conveys such mysteries is marked by

18

hypnotic repetitions and that liberal use of the exclamation-mark so typical of the period. If its effects are 'poetic' they are also, in a loose sense, musical, and in its fatalistic circlings, its motivic repetitions, its tone both fervent and elusive, *Bruges-la-Morte* dwells, like much of the music of the *fin de siècle*, in an inner realm of refined and portentous subjectivity.

Since Hugues's first sightings of Jane culminate in the performance of an opera, it is worth noting that the novel's last scene, with its off-stage procession, tumultuous church-bells and climactic murder, itself resolves a very inward drama in the conventions of grand opera. A fact not lost on the twenty-three-year-old Erich Wolfgang Korngold, whose opera *Die tote Stadt* (premiered simultaneously in Cologne and Hamburg in December 1920) is based indirectly on *Bruges-la-Morte*, and is now the form in which the novel is most widely known. Its immediate source was *Le Mirage*, the four-act theatrical version of *Bruges-la-Morte* which Rodenbach prepared at the end of his life, but never saw staged. In dramatising his book he found himself driven to just those kinds of explication through dialogue that the novel pointedly avoids. Korngold, in following him, and in wrapping the play in his precocious melange of Straussian modernism and Viennese Schmaltz, prolonged and broadened the fame of this recondite novel – but at the cost of what makes it so singular and so unforgettable.

*Alan Hollinghurst*

# PREFATORY NOTE

In this study of passion our other principal aim has been to evoke a Town, the Town as an essential character, associated with states of mind, counselling, dissuading, inducing the hero to act.

And in reality, this town of Bruges, on which our choice fell, does seem almost human. It establishes a powerful influence over all who stay there.

It moulds them through its monuments and its bells.

This is what we have tried to suggest: the Town guiding the action, its urban landscapes not merely as backcloths, as the slightly arbitrary subjects of descriptive passages, but tied to the very events of the book.

That is why, since the scenery of Bruges is directly involved in the story, it is important that they should be reproduced here, interpolated between the pages – quais, deserted streets, old houses, canals, the Béguinage, churches, liturgical objects, the belfry – so that our readers, too, may come under the influence of the Town itself, feel the pervasive presence of the waters from close to, experience for themselves the shadow cast over the text by the tall towers.

# I

The daylight was failing, darkening the corridors of the large, silent house, putting screens of crepe over the windows.

Hugues Viane was preparing to go out, as was his daily habit at the end of the afternoon. Solitary, with nothing to occupy his time, he would spend the whole day in his room, a vast retreat on the first floor whose windows looked out onto the Quai du Rosaire, along which the façade of his house stretched, mirrored in the canal.

He read a little – journals, old books – smoked a lot, and spent hours in reverie at the window open to the grey weather, lost in his memories.

It was five years now that he had been living like this, five years since he had come to settle in Bruges immediately following the death of his wife. Five years already! And he repeated to himself, "Widowed! Widowed! – Bereft!" How abrupt and irrevocable that word sounded! Setting off no responding echo. Well suited for someone left behind from a pair.

The severance had been terrible for him. He had enjoyed love in the lap of luxury, the idyll constantly rekindled by leisure, travel, new countries. Not simply the quiet delights of an exemplary married life, but the passion undiminished, the fever continuing, the kisses scarcely less ardent, two souls in harmony, separate yet together, like the parallel *quais* of a canal, in which their reflections mingle.

Ten years of this happiness, ten years hardly noticed, so quickly had they passed.

Then his young wife had died, just as she reached her

thirtieth year, confined for a few short weeks to her bed, which quickly became her deathbed, an image that would remain with him for ever: faded and white, like the candle burning at her head, the woman he had adored for the beauty of her radiant complexion, of her eyes, black, dilated pupils set in mother of pearl, their darkness contrasting with the amber yellow of her hair, hair which, loosened, covered the whole of her back in long, wavy tresses. The Madonnas of the Primitives have similar flowing locks, descending in calm ripples.

During the last days of her illness, this sheaf had been braided into a long plait and Hugues had cut it off from the recumbent corpse. Is not death merciful in this? It destroys everything, but leaves the hair intact. The eyes, the lips, everything crumbles and disintegrates. The hair does not even lose its colour. It is in that alone that we live on. Even now, after five years, the tresses of his dead wife that he had kept had scarcely faded at all, despite all the salt tears shed.

On that day the bereaved Viane relived his past, but all the more painfully because of the grey November weather in which the bells seemed to scatter the air with sound dust, the dead ashes of the years.

Nevertheless, he decided to go out. Not that he intended to seek some necessary distraction outside, some remedy for his sickness. He did not even want to try. But, as evening approached, he liked to walk, looking for analogies to his grief in deserted canals and ecclesiastical districts.

Going down to the ground floor he saw, along the broad, white passage, the doors normally kept closed standing wide open.

In the silence he called out for his old servant, 'Barbe! . . . Barbe!'

Immediately the woman appeared in the first doorway and, guessing why her master had called her, said, 'Monsieur, I had to do the downstairs rooms today because tomorrow's a holiday.'

'What holiday would that be?' Hugues asked, with a look of irritation.

'What? You don't know, monsieur? The Feast of the Presentation. I have to go to mass and to vespers at the Béguinage. It's like a Sunday. And since I can't work tomorrow, I've tidied up the rooms today.'

Hugues Viane did not conceal his annoyance. She knew very well that he wanted to be present when she performed that task. In those two rooms there were too many treasures, too many souvenirs of Her and of the past to let his servant go about her business there alone. He wanted to be able to keep an eye on her, follow her movements, make sure she took care, check that she showed due respect. When things had to be disturbed for dusting, some precious curio, say, or objects belonging to his dead wife, a cushion, a screen she had made herself, then he wanted to be the one to handle them. He felt that Her touch was everywhere in the intact, unchanging furnishings, sofas, divans, armchairs where she had sat and which preserved the shape, so to speak, of her body. The curtains retained in perpetuity the folds she had given them. As to the mirrors, he felt the clear surfaces needed only the merest touch with a sponge or cloth, so as not to erase her face sleeping in their depths. But what Hugues also wanted to watch over and keep from all harm were the portraits of his poor dead wife, portraits of her at different ages, scattered here and there, on the mantelpiece, the little tables, the walls; and then above all – an accident to this would have shattered his soul – the preserved treasure of that complete head of hair, which he had been unwilling to shut away in some chest of drawers or the darkness of some box – it would have been like consigning it to the tomb – preferring, since it was still alive and of an ageless gold, to leave it displayed, visible, as the immortal part of his beloved!

In order to be able to see them all the time, these locks that were still Her, he had placed them on the piano, silent from

27

now on, in the large, never-changing drawing room. They simply lay there, a cut-off plait, a broken chain, a rope saved from the shipwreck. And to protect the hair from contamination, from the moist atmosphere that could have taken the colour out of it or oxidised its metal, he had had the idea, naive if it had not been touching, of putting it under glass, a transparent casket, a crystal box, the resting place of the bare locks to which he paid homage every day.

For him, as for the silent objects living around, this plait of hair seemed bound up with their existence, seemed the very soul of the house.

Barbe, the old servant, a little sullen, but devoted and meticulous, was aware of all the precautions that had to be taken with these objects and only approached them with trembling. Not very communicative, with her black dress and bonnet of white tulle she had the air of a lay sister. Moreover she often went to the Béguinage to see her only relation, Sister Rosalie, who was a beguine.

From these frequent visits, from these pious habits, she had retained the silence, the gliding step of feet accustomed to the stone flags of a church. And it was for that reason, because she did not surround his grief with noise or laughter, that Hugues Viane had been so satisfied with her since he came to Bruges. He had had no other servant, and Barbe had become indispensable to him, despite her innocent tyranny, her pious, old-maidish ways, her determination to do things after her own fashion, as she had that day when, because of some trifling festival on the morrow, she had turned his rooms upside down, without his knowledge and against his express orders.

Before going out, Hugues waited until she had put the furniture back, checking that everything dear to him was undamaged and in its right place. Then, reassured, with the doors and shutters closed, he set out on his usual twilight walk, even though the heavy drizzle, common in late autumn, did not stop, fine rain, tears falling vertically, weaving moisture, sewing down the air, setting the smooth surface of the canals abristle with needles, capturing and transfixing the soul, like a bird, in the interminable meshes of a watery net!

# II

Every evening Hugues retraced the same route, following the line of the *quais*. His gait was uncertain, slightly hunched already, even though he was only forty. But widowhood had brought an early autumn. His hair was receding, with a copious scattering of grey ash. His faded eyes were fixed on a distant point, a very distant point, beyond life itself.

And how melancholy Bruges was, too, during those late afternoons! That was how he liked the town! It was for its melancholy that he had chosen it and had gone to live there after the great catastrophe. In those happy times when he was travelling round with his wife, living as his fancy took him, a somewhat cosmopolitan life, in Paris, abroad, by the sea, he had passed through the town with her, but its profound melancholy had not had the power to affect their joy. Later on however, once he was alone, he had remembered Bruges and had immediately and instinctively known he must settle there. A mysterious equation gradually established itself. He needed a dead town to correspond to his dead wife. His deep mourning demanded such a setting. Life would only be bearable for him there. It was instinct that had brought him here. He would leave the world elsewhere to its bustle and buzz, to its glittering balls, its welter of voices. He needed infinite silence and an existence that was so monotonous it almost failed to give him the sense of being alive.

In the presence of physical pain, why must we keep silent, tread softly in a sickroom? Why do noises, voices, seem to disturb the dressing and reopen the wound?

30

Those suffering from mental anguish can be hurt by noise too.

In the muted atmosphere of the waterways and the deserted streets, Hugues was less sensitive to the sufferings of his heart, his thoughts of his dead wife were less painful. He had seen her, heard her again more clearly, finding the face of his departed Ophelia as he followed the canals, hearing her voice in the thin, distant song of the bells.

In this way the town, once beautiful and beloved too, embodied the loss he felt. Bruges was his dead wife. And his dead wife was Bruges. The two were united in a like destiny. It was Bruges-la-Morte, the dead town entombed in its stone *quais*, with the arteries of its canals cold once the great pulse of the sea had ceased beating in them.

That evening, as he was making his haphazard way, more than ever the dark memory came to haunt him, emerging from under the bridges, where faces weep tears from invisible springs. The closed houses exhaled a funereal atmosphere, window-panes like eyes clouded in death throes, crow-steps tracing stairways of crepe in the water. He walked along the Quai Vert, the Quai du Miroir and continued out towards the Pont du Moulin, melancholy suburbs lined with poplars. And everywhere the chill spray, the little salt notes of the parish bells on his head, as if sprinkled from an aspergillum for some absolution.

In this solitude, that was both evening and autumnal, with the wind sweeping up the remaining leaves, he felt more than ever the desire to have finished with life and impatience for the tomb. It seemed that a shadow was cast from the towers over his soul, a word of counsel reached him from the old walls, a whispering voice rose from the water – the water coming to him as it came to Ophelia, according to what Shakespeare's gravediggers tell.

More than once he had felt this seduction. He had heard the slow persuasion of the stones, he had truly discerned the nature of things there, not to survive the death all around.

He had thought long and hard about killing himself. That woman, oh, how he had adored her! He still felt her eyes on him, still sought after her voice, now fled to the far horizon. What was it his dead wife had had, to have attached him to her so entirely, to have cut him off from the whole world since she had gone? There is a love, then, which, like the Dead Sea Fruit, leaves nothing but an ineradicable taste of ash in the mouth.

If he had resisted his obsessive thoughts of suicide, then that, too, was for her. Together with the lees of his grief, the residue of his religious childhood had resurfaced. With his tendency towards mysticism, his hope was that life did not end in nothingness and that he would see her again one day. Religion forbade him to kill himself. It would have meant exclusion from heaven and ruled out the vague possibility of seeing her again.

So he lived on. He even prayed, finding consolation in imagining her waiting for him in the gardens of some heaven or other, in dreaming of her in the churches, to the sound of the organ.

That evening, as he made his way round the town, he went into Notre Dame. He liked to go there often because of its sepulchral nature: everywhere, on the walls, on the floor were grave-slabs with skulls, chipped names, eaten away inscriptions as if by stone lips . . . death itself erased by death.

But, alongside them, the emptiness of life was illuminated by the consoling vision of love enduring in death, and that was why Hugues so often made a pilgrimage to this church: the famous tombs, deep within a side chapel, of Charles the Bold and his daughter, Mary of Burgundy. How touching they were! She above all, her fingers placed together, her head on a marble cushion, in a gown of copper, her feet resting against a dog symbolising fidelity, the gentle princess, rigid on the slab of the sarcophagus. Just as his dead wife was resting for ever on his black soul. And the time would come when he in his turn would lie, like Duke Charles, and would rest beside her. Sleeping side by side, in the safe haven of death, if the Christian expectation of being reunited should not be fulfilled for them.

Hugues left Notre Dame more melancholy than ever. Since the time when he usually returned home for his evening meal was approaching, he set off in the direction of his house, seeking within himself the memory of his dead wife in order to apply it to the form of the tomb he had just seen and picture the latter complete with a different face. But the faces of the dead, which are preserved in our memory for a while, gradually deteriorate there, fading like a pastel drawing that has not been kept under glass, allowing the chalk to disperse. Thus, within us, our dead die a second time.

All at once, while he was making an intense mental effort – looking within himself, so to speak – to reconstruct her features, already half erased, Hugues, who usually hardly noticed the rare passers-by, felt a sudden shock on seeing a young woman coming towards him. He had not seen her at first, as she approached from the end of the street, but only when she was quite near.

At the sight of her, he stopped short, as if transfixed; the woman coming in the opposite direction had passed close by him. It was a jolt, an apparition. For a moment Hugues seemed about to swoon. He put his hand over his eyes, as if to ward off a dream. Then, after a moment of hesitation, turning towards the unknown woman as she continued on her way with a slow, fluid gait, he retraced his steps, abandoned the *quai* he had been going along and suddenly started to follow her. He walked quickly, in order to catch up with her, crossing from one pavement to the other, getting closer, looking at her so persistently it would have been unseemly had it not been for the mesmerised look in his eyes. Hugues seemed more and more strange and distraught. Already he had been following her for several minutes, from street to street, now coming closer, as if for a decisive scrutiny, now moving away again, apparently stricken with terror when he came too near to her. He seemed attracted and apprehensive at the same time, like someone trying to make out a face in a deep well . . .

Yes! This time he had definitely recognised her, it was undeniable. That velvety complexion, those eyes, the blackest, dilated pupils set in mother of pearl, they were the same. And as he walked along behind her, the hair emerging at the nape of her neck, from under her black hat and veil, was definitely of a similar gold, the colour of amber and raw silk, of a fluid yellow texture. The same clash between the night-dark eyes and the blazing noon of her hair.

Was his mind giving way? Or was it his retina which, from the effort of retrieving the image of his dead wife, had started to identify passers-by with her. Whilst he was searching for Her face, this woman had abruptly appeared, presenting him with its double, too similar, too alike. A disturbing apparition! An almost frightening miracle of resemblance that went as far as identity.

Everything: her gait, her figure, the rhythm of her body, the expression of her features, the inwardness of her look, things not merely of shape and colour, but expressions of a person's spirituality, movements of their soul – all that was given back to him, had returned, was alive!

With the air of a sleepwalker, Hugues continued to follow her, though mechanically now, without knowing why and without thinking, through the misty labyrinth of the streets of Bruges. Coming to a crossroads, a tangle of streets running in several directions, and walking some way behind, he suddenly lost sight of her – gone, vanished down one or other of these twisting alleys.

He stopped, surveying the distance, scanning empty space, the tears welling up . . .

Oh, how she resembled his dead wife!

# III

This encounter left Hugues's feelings in turmoil. Now, when he thought of his wife, it was the unknown woman from the other evening that he saw. She was his memory of her, brought to life, brought into sharp focus. She seemed to him as close a likeness of his dead wife as possible.

When he went to perform his silent devotions, kissing the relic of her hair or giving rein to his emotions before some portrait, it was no longer his dead wife to whom he related the image, but the living woman who resembled her. Mysterious conformity of these two faces! It was as if fate had taken pity on him, providing his memory with markers, conspiring with him against oblivion, substituting a crisp new print for the one that was fading, already yellowed and mildewed with age.

Hugues's vision of the woman who had disappeared from view was fresh and sharp. He only had to call up the memory of the old *quai* he had been going along the other day, as evening was falling, and a woman coming towards him who had the face of his dead wife. He no longer needed to go back, into the past, the distant past, all he had to do was to think back one or two evenings. Now everything was close, everything was easy. His eye had stored up a fresh image of the beloved face. The recent impression had fused with the old one, each reinforcing the other in a likeness which had almost come to give the illusion of a real presence.

During the days that followed Hugues was a man obsessed. So there was a woman who was absolutely the same as the one he had lost! Having seen her in the street, for a minute he had been visited by the cruel dream that his dead wife was going

39

to return, had returned and was walking towards him, as in the past. The same eyes, the same complexion, the same hair – a complete likeness. A strange caprice of nature and of fate!

He would have liked to see her again. Perhaps he never would. However, just to know that she was near, that he might meet her, made him feel less alone, less of a widower. Is a man truly a widower when his wife is merely absent and briefly returns now and then?

If the woman who resembled her should happen to pass by, he would imagine he had found his dead wife again. In this hope, he went at the same hour of the evening to the area of the town where he had seen her. He walked up and down the old *quai* with its blackened, crow-stepped gables, its windows veiled in muslin curtains from behind which idle women, quickly alert to his comings and goings, watched him. He plunged into the dead streets, the twisting alleys, hoping to see her emerge, abruptly, at the corner of some crossroads.

One week passed in this way, one week of disappointed expectation. It was already fading from his mind when, on the Monday, the very same day he had first encountered her, he saw her again, recognising her at once as she came towards him with the same swaying walk. Even more than the previous time, the likeness seemed to him complete, absolute and truly frightening.

His heart almost stopped from the shock, as if he were about to die, his ears were ringing, his vision was a blur of white muslin, bridal veils, girls in procession to their first communion. Then, very near and black, the shape of the silhouette that was about to pass right next to him.

The woman must have noticed his inner turmoil, for she looked in his direction with an astonished air. Oh that look, recovered, returned from the void! That look he thought he would never see again, which he pictured dissolved in the earth. Now he felt it on him, steady and mild, blossoming anew, caressing him once more. That look which had come

40

from so far away, raised from the tomb, like the look Lazarus must have given Jesus.

Hugues had no will of his own, his whole being was drawn, pulled along in the wake of this apparition. His dead wife was there, in front of him, walking, going away. He had to go after her, approach her, look at her, drink in those rediscovered eyes, rekindle his life from that hair which was made of light. He had to follow her, simply, without question, to the end of the town and to the end of the world.

He did not think about it, he just automatically set off again behind her, quite close this time, breathless with fear of losing her again in this old town with its circuitous, meandering streets.

It certainly never for one moment occurred to him that what he was doing was out of character. Following a woman?! No, it was his *wife* he was following, he was accompanying on this twilight walk, his wife whom he was going to see back to her tomb . . .

All this time Hugues, as if trapped in a magnetic field, as if in a dream, was walking beside or behind the unknown woman without even noticing that they had left the deserted *quais* and reached the shops, the centre of the town, the Grand'Place where the tower of the old Market Hall, huge and black, was defending itself against the invading night with the golden buckler of its clock-face.

The young woman, slim and swift, appeared to be trying to escape this pursuit as she set off down rue Flamande, with its old façades carved and ornamented like ships' poops. But every time she passed a lighted shop window or the spreading halo of a street-lamp, her silhouette appeared in clearer, sharper outline.

Then he saw her abruptly turn across the road and head for the theatre, which had its doors open. She went in.

Hugues did not stop. He had become a passive object, a satellite in tow. The movements of the soul also gather their own momentum. Carried along by his earlier impetus, he too entered the foyer, into which the crowds were flocking. But the vision had vanished. He could not see the young woman anywhere, neither among the people queuing, nor at the box office, nor on the stairs. Where had she disappeared to? Along which corridor? Through which side door? He had definitely seen her go in, there was no possibility of error about that. She must be going to see the performance. She would be in the auditorium in a few minutes, was perhaps already there, sitting in her seat, or in the red darkness of a box. To see her again! To have her clearly in view for a whole evening! He felt his head start to spin at the thought, which was both painful and pleasurable at the same time. But the idea of resisting the suggestion never even occurred to him. Without pausing to think, without considering either the frenetic way he had been behaving for the last hour, or the anomaly of going to a theatre in the deep mourning he was, as always, wearing, he went straight to the box office, asked for a seat and entered the auditorium.

His eye quickly scoured all the seats, the rows of the stalls, the boxes, the balconies, the galleries which were gradually filling, illuminated by the pervasive light of the chandeliers. He could not find her. He felt disconcerted, troubled, sad. What evil fate was mocking him? A hallucination, a face shown to him then snatched away, appearing intermittently, like the moon through the clouds. He waited a while, then looked round again. Latecomers were hurrying to their places in a screech of doors and seats.

She alone was not among them.

He was starting to regret his unthinking action, all the more because people had noticed him, their amazement producing a concentration of opera glasses focused on him which he could not but be aware of. He had no acquaintances, no families he visited, he lived alone. But in this town, its sparse population with so little to occupy it, in this Bruges where

42

everyone knows everyone else, asks about newcomers, tells their neighbours, gets information from them, everyone knew him by sight, at least knew who he was, knew of his noble despair.

It was a surprise, the end of a legend almost. And a triumph for the more malicious among them who had always smiled when people spoke of the inconsolable widower.

At that moment Hugues, influenced by whatever effluvium emanates from a crowd when it is united in collective thought, had the sense of a sin against himself, a noble ideal betrayed, a first crack in the vase of his cult of his dead wife, through which his sorrow, well kept until then, would drain away entirely.

However, the orchestra had just started the overture of the work to be performed. Hugues had seen the title in large capitals on the programme of the man sitting next to him: *ROBERT LE DIABLE*, one of those old-fashioned operas which almost invariably form the staple of the provincial repertory. The violins were just playing the first bars.

Hugues felt even more disturbed. Since the death of his wife, he had not listened to any music at all. He was afraid of the sound of the instruments. Even a street accordion with its acid, asthmatic music could bring tears to his eyes. The organ as well, on Sundays, in Notre Dame or St Walburga's, where it seemed to drape black velvet catafalques of sound over the faithful.

Now the opera music was flooding his brain, the bows were playing on his nerves. His eyes started to smart. Was he going to cry again? He was thinking of leaving, when a strange thought flashed through his mind. The woman whom he had followed, as if in a fit of madness, for the balm of her resemblance, all the way into this theatre, was not here, he was sure of that. But she had gone into the theatre, before his very eyes almost. If, then, she was not in the auditorium, perhaps she was going to appear on the stage?

It was a profanation the very thought of which tore his soul apart. The same face, the face of his Wife herself, on display in the footlights, emphasised by make-up! What if this woman, followed then lost to sight, doubtless through some stage door, were an actress and he was going to see her appear, gesticulating, singing? Ah! Her voice? Would it be the same voice as well, continuing the fiendish resemblance, that rich metallic voice, like silver with a little bronze, which he had never heard again, never?

Hugues felt deeply perturbed at the mere possibility of the coincidence being carried through to the end. He waited, full of apprehension and with a kind of premonition that his suspicions were true.

The acts passed without telling him anything. He did not see her among the singers, nor among the women of the chorus, powdered and painted like wooden dolls. Otherwise he paid no attention to the opera, he had made up his mind to leave after the scene with the nuns, the graveyard setting of which brought him back to his sepulchral thoughts. But suddenly, during the recitative calling up the dead, when the ballerinas, representing nuns raised from the dead, enter in a long file, when Helena starts to move on her tomb and, throwing off shroud and habit, comes back to life, Hugues felt a shock, like a man coming out of a black dream and into an illuminated ballroom where the light flickers in the teetering balance of his vision.

Yes! It was her! She was a dancer, but he did not dwell on that for one moment. The dead woman coming down from the slab of her tomb over there was truly his dead wife. Now she was smiling, stepping forward, holding out her arms.

And even more of a likeness now, so like as to make him weep, with her eyes of a bistre which intensified the shadowy gloom, with her hair plain to see, of a unique gold, like the other woman . . .

A gripping but fleeting apparition on which the curtain soon fell.

Hugues, his mind afire, distraught and elated, made his way home along the *quais*, as if mesmerised by the persistent vision which still opened out its frame full of light before him, even in the blackness of the night . . . Like Faust, reaching out for the mirror in which the divine image of woman is revealed.

# IV

It took no time for Hugues to find out about her. He learnt her name, Jane Scott, from the poster, where she had star billing. She lived in Lille and came to Bruges twice a week to give performances with the company she belonged to.

Dancers hardly have a reputation for being puritan, so one evening, tempted by the melancholy charm of her resemblance, he approached her.

She replied, without appearing surprised and as if she were expecting the encounter, in a voice which moved him to his very soul. Her voice too! The voice of his dead wife, exactly the same, heard once more, a voice worked in the same precious metal. Was the demon of analogy mocking him? Or is there a secret harmony in faces so that for those eyes, for that hair there had to be a matching voice?

Why should she not have his dead wife's voice, since she had her black, dilated pupils in mother of pearl, her hair of rare gold, in an alloy which seemed unique? Now, seeing her from closer, from very close to, there was no difference discernible between his dead wife and the living woman. It left Hugues nonplussed, as did the fact that, despite the powder, the make-up, the heat of the footlights, she still had the same fresh, natural complexion. Nor did she have the free-and-easy bearing common in dancers. She dressed in sober fashion, appeared to be of a reserved and gentle disposition.

Hugues saw her several times, talked to her. The spell of the resemblance worked, though he took care not to go back to the theatre again. That first evening had been a delightful trick of fate. Since she was destined to provide him with the illusion of his dead wife returned from the grave, it was quite right that she should have first appeared to him as a woman risen from the dead and coming down from her tomb in a setting full of magic and moonlight.

But from now on he did not intend to see her like that any more. She was his dead wife become a living woman again, having started anew her quiet life, clothing herself in quiet fabrics. To preserve the illusion, henceforward Hugues only wanted to see the dancer in her everyday clothes, giving her a closer resemblance, a perfect likeness.

Now, whenever she was appearing in Bruges, he often went to see her at the hotel where she stayed. At first he contented himself with the consoling delusion of her face. He searched that face for the features of his dead wife. With a melancholy joy, he would look at her for minutes on end, storing up her lips, her hair, her complexion, tracing them on the stagnant pools of his eyes . . . Exhilaration, rapture from the well he had thought empty and where a presence was now enshrined. The water no longer bare, the mirror come to life!

To enjoy the delusion of her voice, he would sometimes close his eyes, listen to her talking, drink in that sound, almost identical to the life, except for an occasional slight muting, muffling of the words. It was as if his former wife were speaking from behind a drape.

However, there remained a disturbing memory from her appearance on the stage. He had caught a glimpse of her bare arms, her bosom, the supple line of her back, and imagined them now, under her buttoned-up dress.

Curiosity to know her flesh seeped in.

Who can describe the passionate embraces of a loving couple who have been separated for a long time? Here death had been merely an absence, since the same woman had returned.

Looking at Jane, Hugues thought of his dead wife, of the kisses, the caresses of the past. In possessing her he would be

49

possessing his dead wife again. What had seemed finished for good was going to start once more. And he would not even be unfaithful to his Wife, since it would be Her he was making love to in this effigy, Her he was kissing on those lips that were the same as hers.

Thus Hugues came to know fierce and funereal delights. He did not see his passion as a profanation, but as good, so completely had he merged these two women into a single person – lost, found, always loved, in the present as in the past, with eyes in common, tresses undivided, one flesh, one body to which he remained faithful.

Now, every time Jane came to Bruges, Hugues went to see her, either in the late afternoon, before the performance, or, and above all, afterwards, in those long, silent midnights he spent beside her in an ecstasy of pleasure. Despite all appearances – the deep mourning he still wore, the different hotel rooms which remained foreign to him – he gradually managed to persuade himself that the bad years had never existed, that he was at home, with his first wife, the loving couple enjoying the quiet intimacy preceding their lawful embraces.

Those idyllic evenings! An enclosed room, peace within, a couple in accord, sufficient unto themselves, silence, peaceful tranquillity. Their eyes, like nocturnal moths, have forgotten everything – the dark corners, the cold windows, the rain outside, and, in the winter, the bells sounding out the death of the hours – to flutter round in the confined circle of the lamp.

Hugues relived those evenings. The past erased! A new beginning! Time flowing freely on a bed without stone banks ... And it seemed that, living, he was already living in eternity.

# V

Hugues installed Jane in a pleasant house he had leased for her on an esplanade leading to leafy suburbs with windmills.

At the same time he had persuaded her to give up the theatre. In that way he would have her in Bruges all the time, and more to himself. Not for one moment, however, had he considered how absurd a sedate man of his age must look becoming infatuated with a dancer after such inconsolable and widely known grief. To tell the truth, he was not in love with her. All he wanted was to be able to perpetuate the illusion of this mirage. When he took Jane's head in his hands and drew it close to him, it was to look at her eyes, to try and find in them something he had seen in other eyes and which was perhaps floating in Jane's: a nuance, a glint, pearls, blooms whose roots are in the soul.

At other times he would undo her hair, letting it pour over her shoulders, mentally matching them up to absent tresses, as if they were to be spun together.

Jane was baffled by Hugues's bizarre behaviour, his mute contemplation. She recalled his unexplained sadness, at the beginning of their affair, when she had told him her hair was dyed, and the intensity with which he observed her to see if she was keeping it the same shade.

'I want to stop dyeing it,' she had said one day.

He had been extremely disturbed at the idea and insisted she kept her hair the bright gold colour he liked so much. As he said that, he had taken it in his hands, stroking it, running his fingers through it, like a miser digging his hands into the treasure he has recovered.

And he had babbled confusedly, 'Don't change anything . . . it's because you're like that that I love you. Oh, you don't know, you can't ever know what I touch when I touch your hair . . .'

He seemed about to say more, then stopped short, as if on the edge of a precipice of revelation.

Since she had come to live in Bruges, he went to see her almost every day, generally spending his evenings with her, sometimes eating there too, despite the fact that this put his old servant, Barbe, in a bad mood and she would spend the next day moaning about having wasted her time preparing a meal and waiting for him. Barbe pretended to believe he really had eaten at a restaurant, but at bottom she remained sceptical. This was no longer the old punctual, reclusive master she knew.

Hugues went out often, dividing his time between his house and Jane's.

He preferred to go there towards evening, from his old habit of not going out until the end of the afternoon, and also so as not to be too conspicuous as he made his way to the house he had deliberately chosen in a quiet district. He had felt no shame for himself, no inner blushes, because he knew the motive, the reason for this transposition which was not only an excuse, but absolution, justification before his dead wife and, almost, before God. But he had to reckon with the prudishness of provincial society. How can a man not feel some concern about what other people think, their hostility or respect, when all the time he feels their eyes on him, touching him, so to speak?

Above all in this Catholic town of Bruges, where morality is so strict! The tall towers in their stone habits cast their shadow everywhere. Contempt for the secret roses of the flesh, a pervasive glorification of chastity seems to emanate from the innumerable convents. On every street corner, cased in wood and glass, are statues of the Blessed Virgin in velvet cloaks, surrounded by fading paper flowers and holding in their hands a scroll unfurled proclaiming, for their part, 'I am the Immaculate Conception.'

There passion, sexual relations outside marriage, are always works of evil, the road to hell, the sin of the sixth and ninth commandments which makes women lower their voices in the confessional and blush with shame.

Hugues was aware of this strictness and had avoided giving offence. But in the narrowness of provincial life nothing goes unnoticed. Soon, without knowing, he had aroused pious indignation. But faith, when scandalised, likes to resort to irony, just as the cathedral mocks and laughs at the devil with its masks and gargoyles. Once the widower's liaison with the dancer was noised abroad he became, without realising it, the laughing stock of the town. No one was unaware of it. Doorstep chatter, idle gossip, tittle-tattle, all was greeted with the prurience of pious bigots – the weed of scandal which springs up between all the paving stones in dead towns.

People found his affair all the more amusing because they had known about his long despair, his mourning without respite, all his thoughts gathered and tied in a bouquet for a tomb. So that was where the grief you would have thought eternal ended up!

They had all been mistaken, including the poor widower himself, who had doubtless been bewitched by a strumpet. She used to be a dancer, had been on the stage. They pointed her out to each other as she went past, laughing, slightly outraged at her appearance of respectability which, they found, was contradicted by her swaying walk and her yellow hair. They even knew where she lived and that the widower went to see her every evening. Not long and they would be putting out a timetable of his itinerary . . .

Sitting at their windows in the emptiness of their idle afternoons, the good women of Bruges, ever curious, watched him as he went past, keeping him under observation in those little mirrors, called *busybodies*, you see fixed to the outside of the window-frames on all the houses: slanting mirrors reflecting the streets in dubious section, glinting traps that capture, without their knowledge, all the little stratagems of the passers-by – their gestures, their smiles, a momentary thought revealed in their eyes – and relay it to the inside of the house where someone is keeping watch.

Thus, thanks to the treachery of the mirrors, they soon knew all Hugues's comings and goings, every detail of the semi-concubinage in which he was living with Jane. The delusion in which he persisted, his naive precaution of only going to see her as evening was falling, made the liaison, which had offended people at first, look slightly ridiculous and the indignation turned to laughter.

Hugues did not suspect anything. He continued to go out as daylight was failing to make his deliberately roundabout way to the nearby suburb.

How less sorrowful they were now, those twilight walks! He went through the town, across the centuries-old bridges, along the sepulchral *quais* where the water sighs. Every time the bells, in the evening, were tolling for some office for the dead to be held the next day. Oh, those bells ringing out, but so departed, so to speak, already so far away from him, as if pealing under other skies . . .

And however much the overflow from the gutters continued to drip, the cold tears ooze out on the underside of the bridges, the poplars beside the water tremble like the lament of some thin, inconsolable spring, Hugues was deaf to the sorrow of things around. He no longer saw the town as a rigid corpse swathed in the myriad bandages of its canals.

The former town, Bruges-la-Morte, the dead town of which he seemed to be the widower, now only brushed him with the merest glaze of melancholy. Consoled, he walked through its silent streets as if Bruges, too, had risen from its

tomb and were presenting itself to him as a new town which happened to resemble the old one.

And as he made his way each evening to see Jane, there was not one spark of remorse, not, for one moment, a sense of betrayal, of great love sunk to parody, of sorrow abandoned, not even the little shiver that runs through a woman the first time she pins a red rose to the black of her widow's weeds.

# VI

Hugues was deep in thought. What indefinable power there is in resemblance!

It corresponds to the two contradictory needs of human nature: habit and novelty. Habit is the law, the very rhythm of our being, and Hugues had practised it with an intensity which determined his destiny irremediably. Having spent ten years at the side of a woman who remained dear to him, he could not accustom himself to life without her, continued to concern himself with his absent wife and seek her features in other faces.

The desire for novelty, on the other hand, is no less instinct-ive. We tire of blessings even, if they remain the same, can only enjoy our happiness, as our health, by contrast. And love, too, resides in discontinuity.

And it is precisely resemblance which reconciles these two within us, balances them, joins them at some undefined point. Resemblance is the horizon where habit and novelty meet.

In love, the way this subtle mechanism operates is princi-pally in the charm of a new woman appearing who resembles our former lover and Hugues, whom solitude and grief had long since made sensitive to these nuances of the soul, enjoyed it with increasing delight. After all, was it not an innate feeling for desirable analogies that had brought him to Bruges when his wife died?

He possessed what one might call a 'sense of resemblance', an extra sense, frail and sickly, which linked things to each other by a thousand tenuous threads, relating trees to the Virgin Mary, creating a spiritual telegraphy between his soul and the grief-stricken towers of Bruges.

That was why he had chosen Bruges, Bruges, from which the sea had withdrawn, as his great happiness had withdrawn from him. That in itself was an example of the phenomenon of resemblance, and because his mind would be in harmony with the greatest of the Grey Towns.

How melancholy is the grey of the streets of Bruges, where every day is like All Saints' Day! A grey that seems to be made by mixing the white of the nuns' head-dresses with the black of the priests' cassocks, constantly passing here and pervasive. A mystery this grey, this perpetual half mourning.

Everywhere along the streets the façades shade into infinity. Some are of a pale green wash, or faded brickwork, repointed in white. But beside them are others of black, austere charcoal drawings, burnt etchings whose inks moderate, compensate for the somewhat lighter neighbouring tones. But what emanates from the whole is still grey, drifting, spreading along the alignment of the walls, along the *quais*.

The sound of the bells also seems blackish. Muffled, blurred in the air, it arrives as a reverberation which, equally grey, moves along in sluggish, bobbing waves over the waters of the canals.

And the waters themselves, despite all the reflections – patches of blue sky, tiles on the roofs, snowy swans sailing along, green poplars on the banks – coalesce in paths of colourless silence.

In Bruges a miracle of the climate has produced some mysterious chemistry of the atmosphere, an interpenetration which neutralises too-bright colours, reduces them to a uniform tone of reverie, to an amalgam of greyish drowsiness.

It is as if the frequent mists, the veiled light of the northern skies, the granite of the *quais*, the incessant rain, the rhythm of the bells had combined to influence the colour of the air; and also, in this aged town, the dead ashes of time, the dust from the hourglass of the years spreading its silent deposit over everything.

That is why Hugues had decided to take refuge there, in order to feel his last energies silt up, slowly but surely grind to a halt beneath this fine dust of eternity which would turn his soul grey as well, the colour of the town.

Now, in a sudden and almost miraculous about-turn, his sense of resemblance had acted on him again, but in the opposite direction. How, by what trick of fate in this town so far removed from his earliest memories, had this face suddenly appeared which was to revive them all?

However this bizarre coincidence had come about, henceforward Hugues gave himself up to the intoxicating effects of Jane's resemblance to his dead wife, just as in the past he had rejoiced in the resemblance between the town and himself.

# VII

During the several months since he had met Jane, nothing had happened to mar the lie which had given him new life. And how his life had changed! He was no longer sad. He no longer had the feeling of solitude in an immense void. Jane had restored to him the woman he had loved and who had seemed for ever so far beyond reach. He had found her again, he saw her in Jane, just as you see a second moon traced on the surface of the water. Up to now there had not been the least ripple, the least disturbance in a rough wind, to impair the perfection of this mirror image.

It was so completely his wife to whom he continued to make love in the simulacrum of this likeness that he never for one moment felt he was being unfaithful to her memory or to his cult of her. Every morning, just as on the morning after her death, he made his devotions before the relics of her he had preserved, as if at the stations of the cross of love. As soon as he got up, he spent a long time in the silent shadow of the rooms, with blinds half-open, among furniture that was never disturbed, moved to tears before the portraits of his wife: here a photograph of her when she was a girl, not long before they got engaged; in the middle of a panel a large pastel portrait, the reflecting glass of which alternately hid and showed her, an intermittent silhouette; there, on a little table, another photograph in a niello frame, a portrait from her last years, when she already looked ailing, like a wilting lily . . . Hugues placed his lips on them and kissed them, as if they were communion plates or holy reliquaries.

Every morning he also contemplated the crystal casket in

which his dead wife's tresses lay, always manifest. But he hardly ever lifted the lid. He would not have dared pick them up or run his fingers through them. Those locks were sacred, the very body of his dead wife, the part that had escaped the tomb to sleep a better sleep in that glass coffin. But they were still dead, since they had come from a dead body, and they must never be touched. It must be enough to look at them, to know they were intact, to make sure they were always there, those locks on which the whole life of the house perhaps depended.

Thus Hugues spent long hours reviving his memories while, in the enclosed silence of the room, the chandelier above his head sprinkled the fine rain of a faint lament from the aspergillum of its shivering crystal.

Then he went to see Jane, as if she were the last station of his devotions, Jane, who possessed those locks, entire and living, Jane who was like the most true-to-life of the portraits of his dead wife. One day even, in order to delude himself with an even more detailed correlation, Hugues had had a bizarre idea with which he was immediately taken. It was not only small objects of his wife's that he had preserved, trinkets, portraits, he had wanted to keep everything, as if she had merely gone away for a while. Nothing had been thrown or given away, nothing sold. Her bedroom was kept ready, as if she might return at any moment, tidy, the same as ever, with a fresh consecrated boxwood bough each Palm Sunday. Her linen was all there, piled up in drawers full of lavender bags to keep it intact in its yellowed immobility. Her clothes, too, all her old dresses were hanging in the wardrobes, silks and poplins void of gesture.

Hugues liked to go and look at them sometimes, determined not to forget anything, to perpetuate his grief . . .

Like religion, love needs its little practices to keep it alive. One day a strange desire came to him and immediately haunted him until it could be realised: to see Jane in one of those gowns, dressed as his dead wife had been. To see Jane, already such a close likeness, adding, to the sameness of her face, the sameness of one of those gowns, which he had seen in the past moulded by an identical figure. It would make her even more his wife come back from the grave.

Oh, that heavenly moment when Jane would come towards him dressed like that, a moment which would abolish time and reality, which would allow him to forget everything!

Once the idea had found its way into his head, it became fixed, obsessive, asserting itself.

He made up his mind. One morning he called his old servant to get her to bring down from the attic the trunk he was going to use to carry some of her precious dresses.

'Monsieur is going on a journey?' Barbe asked. Finding no explanation for the new style of life – going out, eating out, staying out – adopted by her master, who used to keep himself shut off from the world, she was beginning to suspect him of entertaining fads.

He got her to help him take down and go through the dresses, also to keep them free of the clouds of dust that quickly blew up in the wardrobes which had remained so long undisturbed.

He chose two dresses, the last two his dead wife had bought, and carefully laid them in the trunk, smoothing out the skirts, patting down the pleats.

Barbe had no idea what he was doing, but she was shocked to see him split up the wardrobe no one had ever touched. Was it going to be sold? So she asked:

'What would poor Madame say?'

Hugues stared at her. He had gone pale. Could she have guessed? Could she know?

'What do you mean?' he asked.

'I think,' Barbe replied, 'that in my village, in Flanders, when you don't sell a dead person's clothes immediately, the week of the funeral, you must keep them for the rest of your natural life, or the dead person will stay in purgatory until you die yourself.'

'There's no need to concern yourself,' said Hugues, relieved. 'I have no intention of selling anything. Your legend is quite right.'

Still Barbe was dumbfounded when she saw him a little later, despite what he had said, have the trunk loaded on a cab and drive off.

Hugues did not know how to convey his crazy idea to Jane, for – out of a kind of tact, a sense of propriety towards his wife – he had never spoken to her about his past, nor even alluded to the sweet and cruel likeness he sought in her.

When the trunk arrived, Jane skipped up and down, uttering little cries. What a surprise! He really was too good to her! What was it? Presents? A dress?

'Yes, some dresses,' Hugues replied mechanically.

'Oh, how kind. So there's more than one?'

'Two.'

'What colour? Quick, let me see.'

She went up to him, holding out her hand for the key.

Hugues did not know what to say. He did not dare speak for fear of betraying himself, of explaining the morbid desire to which he had yielded like a man accustomed to acting on impulse.

When the trunk was opened, Jane exhumed the dresses and rapidly surveyed them, disappointment immediately appearing on her features.

'What an ugly style! And that pattern in the silk, it's old, old! Wherever did you manage to buy dresses like that? And those pleats in the skirt, no one's been wearing those for ten years. Is this your idea of a joke?'

Hugues was still at a loss for words, painfully aware of his mistake. He looked for something he could say, not the truth but some other, plausible explanation. He was beginning to see how ridiculous his idea was, but still it held him in its grip.

Oh, if only she would agree! If only she would put on one of those dresses! Even if just for a moment, for him that moment, during which he would see her dressed in the same way as the other woman, would bring the likeness to a climax, would allow him the infinite luxury of forgetting.

He explained to her, in a cajoling voice, that, yes, they were old dresses . . . he'd inherited them . . . from a relation . . . he'd thought it might be fun . . . to see her in one of those old dresses. It was crazy, but he wanted to see her like that . . . just for a minute.

Jane, somewhat bewildered, laughed, and kept turning the two dresses over and over, delighting in the material – a rich silk, scarcely faded – but still not knowing what to make of the strange and slightly ridiculous style which, nevertheless, had once been the height of fashion and elegance.

Hugues persisted.

'But you'll think I look ugly!'

At first baffled by his whim, Jane eventually came to find the idea of dressing up in the cast-offs amusing. Laughing playfully, she took off her negligée and, her arms bare, adjusting the camisole that covered her corset, folding it back, as she did the lace of her chemise, put on one of the dresses, a low-cut dress . . . Standing in front of the mirror, Jane laughed to see herself like that, exclaiming, 'I look like an old portrait!'

She postured and twisted, then, lifting up her skirts, climbed onto the table to see herself fully, laughing all the time, her breast shaking, part of her chemise coming loose and sticking out from the bodice over the bare flesh, less chaste than the flesh itself, suggesting the intimacy of lingerie . . .

Hugues gazed at her. This moment, which he had dreamt of as supreme, a culmination, seemed polluted, vulgar. Jane was enjoying herself. Now she wanted to try on the other dress and, in a fit of wild exuberance, started to dance with a multiplicity of entrechats, slipping back into the choreography of the stage.

Hugues was more and more ill at ease. He had the feeling
he was watching a distressing masquerade. It was the first time
the spell cast by the physical likeness had not been strong
enough. It was still working, but in reverse. Without the
resemblance, he would have found Jane merely vulgar, with it
she gave him the horrible feeling he was seeing his dead wife
again, but degraded, despite the sameness of face and dress –
the feeling you get on the evening of some religious festival
when you meet the women who represented the Virgin
Mary and the saints in the procession, still wearing the mantle,
the holy costumes, but slightly drunk, reduced to a mystical
carnival beneath street lights like wounds bleeding in the
darkness.

# VIII

On the morning of one Sunday in March Barbe was told by her master that he was not going to take either dinner or supper at home and that she was therefore free until the evening. It was Easter Sunday and she was delighted at this since, her free day coinciding with one of the great feast days, she could go to the Béguinage for the services – high mass, vespers, the benediction – and spend the other time with her relation, Sister Rosalie, who lived in one of the principal convent houses of the precinct.

Visiting the Béguinage was one of Barbe's greatest, indeed one of her only joys. Everyone there knew her. She had a number of friends among the beguines and dreamt of going there herself in her old age, when she had accumulated some savings, to take the veil and finish her life like all the other – happy! – women she saw with their faces of old ivory enshrouded in a cornet.

On that young March morning especially she rejoiced to be making her way to her beloved Béguinage, still managing a sprightly step in her large, black, hooded cloak, swinging like a bell. Distant peals, parish bells in unison, seemed to ring out in rhythm with her steps, and mingling with them every quarter, the tinny, quavering music of the carillon, like a tune on a glass harmonica . . .

The first signs of spring foliage gave the suburb a country air and, although Barbe had been in service in the town for over thirty years, the memory of her village had remained, as with all women like her, evergreen in her mind. Still a peasant at heart, she was moved by the sight of a patch of grass or a few leaves . . .

What a fine morning! And as she made her way with jaunty step in the bright sunshine, responding to the call of a bird, the scent of young growth in this district with its suggestion of the rustic, the verdant beauty spots of the *Minnewater* – the lake of love, as it might be translated, or, even better, the waters where people are in love! – there, at the sight of the sleepy pool with its water lilies like the hearts of girls at their first communion, its grassy banks dotted with small flowers, its tall trees, its windmills gesticulating on the horizon, Barbe once more had the illusion she was journeying back, across the fields, to her childhood . . .

She was also a devout soul, with that Flanders faith which retains something of Spanish Catholicism, in which qualms of conscience and terror are stronger than the assurance of belief, which goes more in fear of hell than in hope of heaven. Yet it also has a love of decoration, of the sensuousness of flowers, incense, rich fabrics, which is peculiar to that race. That was why the humble mind of the old servant was already in raptures at the prospect of the splendour of the holy offices as she crossed the arched bridge leading to the Béguinage and entered the mystic precinct.

Here, already, the silence of a church. In here even the sound of the brooklets trickling into the lake outside was like the murmur of lips in prayer. And everywhere walls, the walls surrounding the houses, as white as the cloths on the holy altar; in the middle grass, thick and luxuriant, a Jan van Eyck meadow with a sheep grazing like the Paschal Lamb.

Lanes with the names of female saints and blessed martyrs turn and fork, entangle and straighten out, forming a hamlet from the Middle Ages, a small town apart within another town and even more dead. So empty, so quiet, with a silence so pervasive you walk softly, you talk in a low voice, as you do in a place where someone is ill.

If, by chance, some passer-by should approach and make a noise, you have the feeling of something abnormal, something

72

sacrilegious. The only ones who really belong there are a few beguines, walking with steps that scarcely brush the ground in that dead atmosphere, since they seem to glide rather than walk, swans rather than women, sisters to the white swans on the long canals. Some, late, were hurrying under the elms growing on the raised strips of grass, as Barbe made her way towards the church, from which the echo of the organ and the chanting of the mass could already be heard. She entered at the same time as the beguines, who went to sit in their choir-stalls, the double row of carved panelling by the chancel. The head-dresses were superimposed, one over the other, all the linen wings immobile, white, dappled with red and blue when the sun passed across the stained-glass windows. From the distance Barbe observed, with an envious eye, the kneeling group of the sisters of the community, brides of Christ and servants of God, hoping that, one day, she too would be one of them . . .

She had gone to sit in one of the side-aisles of the church, among a few others, laymen and laywomen like her: old men, children, poor women who had lodgings in the Béguinage, which was becoming depopulated. Barbe, who could not read, told the fat beads of her rosary, praying loud and clear, at times glancing at her cousin, Sister Rosalie, who occupied the second place in the stalls after the Reverend Mother.

How beautiful the church was, ablaze with the lighted candles! At the offertory Barbe went to buy a little candle from the sacristan who was standing beside a triangular frame of wrought-iron, where her offering, too, was soon burning.

From time to time she turned to see how far her candle, which she could recognise among the others, had burned down.

Oh, how happy she was! And how right the priests were to say that the church is the house of God. Especially at the Béguinage, where it was some of the sisters who sang from the rood-loft, with voices as sweet as only the angels can have.

Barbe never tired of hearing the harmonium, the canticles which unfolded in pure white, like fine linen.

However, now the mass was over, the lights were extinguished.

The beguines all went out together in a shimmer of cornets, a flock rising, studding the green garden for a moment with the white of spread wings, of gulls taking off. Barbe followed Sister Rosalie, but at a distance, out of a sort of respectful discretion, then hurried up when she saw her go into her house, entering it herself a moment later.

Several of the beguines occupy each of the dwellings that make up the community, three or four in one, up to twenty in another. Sister Rosalie's house was one of the larger ones and, at the moment when Barbe entered, all the sisters, hardly had they come back from church, were chatting, laughing and calling out to each other in the vast hall of the workroom. Because it was a feast day the baskets of needlework, the squares of lace had been tidied away. Some of the sisters were examining the plants in the garden outside the building, checking the growth in the beds with their boxwood borders. Others, some of them young, were showing the presents they had received, Easter eggs with sugar frosting. Barbe, a little intimidated, followed her cousin everywhere round the rooms, the parlours where there were crowds of other visitors, afraid of finding herself alone, of appearing to intrude, waiting, in a quiver of anxiety, to be asked to stay for lunch. It was customary, but still! What if too many relatives had come today and there were not enough room?

Barbe was reassured when Sister Rosalie came with an invitation from the Mother Superior. Her cousin then excused herself, saying she was very busy and would have to leave her by herself for a while. The beguines each take a turn at running the household for a week, and this was hers.

'We'll have a talk after lunch,' she went on. 'Especially as I've something serious to tell you.'

'Something serious?' Barbe asked, aghast. 'Then tell me straight away.'

'I haven't time . . . later . . .'

She slipped away down the corridors, leaving Barbe filled with consternation. Something serious? What could it be? Bad news? But there was nothing left that was dear to her, no one but her sole cousin.

So it must be something about herself. What could she be criticised for? What was she being accused of? She had never been guilty of the least dishonesty, not even for a farthing. When she went to confession, she genuinely did not know what to say, what sin to charge herself with.

Barbe continued to be consumed with anxiety. Sister Rosalie had looked so grave when she had spoken to her, almost strict. The great joy she had felt at this day had vanished. She no longer felt like laughing or joining in the groups across the room who were enjoying themselves, gossiping, examining the pieces of lace that were in progress, some new pattern emerging from the inextricable threads on the bobbins.

Sitting on her chair alone, apart from the rest, she spent her time thinking of the unknown matter Sister Rosalie was going to reveal to her.

When they had sat down at the table in the long refectory, after grace had been said, Barbe managed to eat her soup, but only just, and without real pleasure, while she saw all around her the healthy, pink-faced beguines and some other guests, relatives like her, do justice to this doubly special meal: for a Sunday and for a feast day. Wine was served, wine from Touraine, oily and golden, wine used for communion. Barbe emptied the glass that had been poured for her, imagining she could drown her worries. She got a headache.

The meal seemed interminable. When it was over she ran straight to Sister Rosalie, a questioning look on her face. The beguine noticed her distress and quickly tried to reassure her.

'It's nothing Barbe. Come now, there's no need to be alarmed.'

'What is it?'

'Nothing. Nothing very serious. Some advice I have to give you.'

'Oh, you did frighten me . . .'

'When I say nothing serious, I mean nothing serious at the moment. But it could become serious. This is what it is: it might be necessary for you to change your employer.'

'Change my employer? But why ever? I've been with M. Viane for five years now. I'm attached to him because I've seen him when he was very unhappy. And he depends on me. He's the most respectable man in the world.'

'Oh, you poor thing, how naive you are. No, he's not the most respectable man in the world.'

Barbe went pale and asked, 'What do you mean? What has my master done that's wrong?'

Sister Rosalie told her the story that had gone all over the town, even reaching the calm precincts of the Béguinage: the immoral behaviour of the widower people had previously admired for his poignant and inconsolable grief. Well, now he had consoled himself, and in an abominable manner! Now he was visiting a loose woman, a former dancer from the theatre . . .

Barbe was trembling. With Sister Rosalie's every word one more spark of inner resistance was stifled. She looked up to her cousin, and from her lips these revelations, however offensive, however unbelievable they might be to her, took on a note of authority. So that was the cause of all the changes in his way of life which she could not understand, his frequent absences, his comings and goings, eating out, returning home late, staying away overnight . . .?

'Have you considered, Barbe,' Sister Rosalie went on, 'that a respectable, Christian servant cannot continue in service with a man who has become a libertine?'

That word was too much for Barbe. It wasn't possible! She exclaimed. A pack of lies! And Sister Rosalie had been taken in by them. Such a good master, who adored his wife! A master whom she still saw, with her very own eyes, go and cry before the portraits of his dead wife every morning, who watched over her hair better than any relic.

'It is as I told you,' Sister Rosalie replied calmly. 'I know everything. I even know the house where this woman lives. It's on my way into town and I've seen M. Viane go in there more than once.'

That clinched it. It seemed to take the wind out of Barbe's sails. She said nothing but remained immersed in thought, frowning, with a deep furrow down the middle of her forehead.

Then she spoke these simple words: 'I'll think about it,' as her cousin, called to her duties in the pantry, took leave of her for a while.

The old servant sat there, bemused, drained of energy, her thoughts confused at this revelation which threatened to thwart all her hopes and frustrate all her plans for the future.

In the first place she was attached to her master and would be sorry to have to leave him.

And then, where else would she find a position which was so good, so easy and paid so well? In that bachelor household she would have been able to build up her savings until she had the little dowry that was indispensable if she were to end her days here in the Béguinage. But Sister Rosalie was right. She could not stay any longer with a man whose conduct scandalised his fellow-citizens.

She was already aware that you could not work in the households of the ungodly – people who did not pray, did not observe the laws of the church, the fast-days, Lent – and the same held for libertines. They even committed the worst sin, the one the preachers in their sermons and retreats threatened most with the fires of hell. And Barbe quickly suppressed even this distant connection with Lust, at the very name of which she crossed herself.

What to do? Throughout vespers and the benediction, for which they had returned to the church with the rest of the community, Barbe remained perplexed. She prayed to the Holy Ghost for enlightenment, and her prayers were answered for, as she came out, she had reached a decision. Since it was a thorny problem, one that was beyond her, she would go straight to her usual confessor, at Notre Dame, and obediently follow his ruling.

The priest, to whom she told everything she had just learnt, had known this simple, honest woman for years. She was so quick to torment herself with scruples that her poor, humble soul seemed truly crowned with thorns. He tried to calm her and made her promise not to do anything hasty. Even if what people were saying about her master were true and he was involved in an illicit liaison, there were still important distinctions to be made as far as she was concerned. As long as the meetings took place outside the house, she should ignore them, or at least not let them upset her. If, unfortunately, the woman in question should come to her master's house, to see him, to dine or whatever, then she could no longer be party to his debauchery, should resign her position and depart.

Barbe got him to repeat the distinction twice, then, having finally understood it, slipped out of the confessional, left the church after a short prayer and headed back towards the Quai du Rosaire, from which she had set off in such a happy mood that morning and which she felt in her bones she would have to quit sooner or later . . .

Oh how difficult it is to remain joyful for long! She made her way back along the dead streets, remembering wistfully the green suburb in the dawn, the mass, the pure white canticles, everything on which night was falling. She thought, too, of departures to come, of new faces, of her master in a state of

mortal sin. And she saw herself, now without hope of finishing her life in the Béguinage, dying on an evening like this, alone, in the almshouse with the windows that look out onto the canal . . .

# IX

Hugues had suffered a great disillusionment since the day he had had the strange caprice of getting Jane to put on one of his dead wife's outmoded dresses. He had gone too far. By trying to fuse the two women into one he had only succeeded in lessening the resemblance. As long as they were kept at a distance, with the mists of death between them, the illusion remained possible. Brought too close together, the differences emerged.

At first, dazzled by the discovery of the same face, his emotion had been a willing accomplice. Then, little by little, by trying to extend the parallel to smaller and smaller details, he had ended up tormenting himself over nuances.

Resemblances are always in the general outline alone, in the whole. If one insists on focusing on details, everything differs. Hugues, without realising he had changed his way of looking at her, subjecting her to a more minute comparison, blamed Jane and assumed it was she who was transformed.

True, she still had the same eyes. But if the eyes are the windows of the soul, then it was certainly a different soul that appeared in them than had in those, still present, of his dead wife. Jane, quiet and reserved at first, was gradually letting herself go. A whiff of the theatre, of backstage reappeared. Intimacy had encouraged her to return to her free-and-easy behaviour, her boisterous and unrestrained high spirits, her old habit of neglecting her appearance, of going around all day in the house with her negligée untied and her hair unkempt. It offended Hugues's sense of refinement. Still he continued to go to see her, trying to grasp the mirage which was fading.

Those tedious hours! Morose evenings! He needed that voice, still drank its dark waves, at the same time pained by the things it said.

Jane, for her part, was tiring of his black moods, his long silences. Now, when he arrived towards evening, she was still out, not yet returned from strolling round the town, making purchases in the shops, trying on dresses. He came to see her at other times as well, in broad daylight, in the morning or afternoon. Often she was out, not wanting to stay at home any more, bored with her house, always out in the streets. Where did she go? As far as Hugues knew, she had no women friends. He waited for her. He did not like to be there alone, he preferred to walk round the neighbourhood until she came back. Restless, sad, fearful of people's looks, he wandered aimlessly, drifting along, crossing from one pavement to the other, came to the nearby *quais*, walked along beside the water, found himself in symmetrical squares with the sad lament of trees, plunged into the tangle of grey streets.

Oh, that ever-present grey of the streets of Bruges!

Hugues felt himself more and more in thrall to this greyness. He succumbed to the influence of the diffuse silence, the emptiness without passers-by – just a few old women, in black cloaks, their heads under their hoods, who were returning, like shades, from having lit a candle in the Chapel of the Holy Blood. It is a strange thing, but you never see so many old women as in old towns. They go on their way, already the colour of earth, aged and silent, as if they had used up their ration of words ... Hugues scarcely noticed them, going where chance took him, too absorbed in his old sorrow and his present cares. Like an automaton, he returned to Jane's house. Still no one there.

He set off once more, hesitated, went this way and that through the atrophied streets and came, without realising it, to the Quai du Rosaire. He decided to go in; he would not go to see Jane until later, until the evening. He sat down in an armchair, tried to read, then, a moment later, drowning in solitude, overcome by the chill silence of those long corridors, he went out again.

Evening . . . it was drizzling, fine rain spinning out, quickening, skewering his soul . . . Hugues was a prisoner once more, haunted by the face, impelled towards Jane's house. He set off, drew near, turned back, seized all of a sudden with a need to be alone, afraid now that she might be waiting for him at home and not wanting to see her.

With swift steps, he set off in the opposite direction, entering the old districts, wandering without knowing where, bemused, pitiful, in the mire. The rain was coming faster, winding off its threads, tangling its web, the meshes narrower and narrower, an impalpable and moist net in which Hugues felt himself gradually weakening. He started to remember once more . . . He thought of Jane. What could she be doing, outside, at a time like this, in this mournful weather? He thought of his dead wife . . . What was becoming of her? Oh, her poor grave . . . the wreaths and flowers ruined in these downpours . . .

And the bells were ringing, so pale, so far away. How far away the town is! You would think it, too, is no more, has melted away, gone, drowned in the rain which has submerged it completely . . . A matching sadness! It is for Bruges-la-Morte that, from the highest surviving bell-towers, the parish chimes still fall and grieve!

# X

As Hugues felt his touching lie slip away from him, so he turned back again towards the Town, uniting his soul with it, turning to that other parallel which he had already used – when he had first been widowed and come to Bruges – to occupy his grief. Now that Jane no longer appeared absolutely identical to his dead wife, he once more began to resemble the town. He felt at ease on his constant monotonous walks round its empty streets.

For it had come to the point where he was incapable of staying in, fearful of the solitude of his home, of the wind weeping in the chimneys, of the memories multiplying around him, like so many eyes fixed on him. He spent most of the day outside, aimless, bewildered, uncertain of Jane and of his own feelings for her.

Did he really love her? And she? Was it indifference or was it infidelity she was concealing? The nagging pain of uncertainty! The melancholy of the close of these all-too-brief winter afternoons! Drifts of mist gathering. He felt the pervasive fog flooding his soul as well, all his thoughts blurred, drowned in grey lethargy.

Oh, Bruges in winter, at evening!

The town reasserted its influence over him: the lesson in silence from the motionless canals, their calm matching the presence of noble swans; the example of resignation given by the mute *quais*; above all the counsel of piety and austerity falling from the high belfries of Notre Dame and Saint Sauveur, always in view, closing the perspective. Instinctively he lifted his eyes up to them, as if to find refuge there, but the towers mocked his wretched love. 'Look at us,' they seemed to say. 'We are of the Faith alone. Stern, with no smiling sculpture, like airy citadels we rise up towards God. We are the military bell-towers. And the Devil has exhausted his arrows firing at us.'

Yes, Hugues would have liked to be like that. Simply a tower rising above the world. But he could not boast, as did the bell-towers of Bruges, of having thwarted the efforts of the devil. On the contrary, the devouring passion from which he suffered, like a man possessed, could well be seen as a snare of the devil.

He recalled stories of satanism he had read. Was there not some truth in the fear of occult forces and magic spells?

And was all this not the result of a pact that called for blood and would lead him to some dramatic end? There were moments when Hugues felt as if the shadow of death had come near.

He had tried to evade Death, to triumph over it and deride it by the specious artifice of a likeness. Death, perhaps, would have its revenge.

But he could still escape, exorcise himself in time. And from the districts of the great mystic town through which he made his way, he lifted his eyes up once more towards the merciful towers, the consolation of the bells, the compassion of the statues of the Blessed Virgin, which, on every street corner, open their arms from the depths of a niche, among tapers and roses under a dome, for all the world like dead flowers in a glass coffin.

Yes, he would throw off the evil yoke. He repented. He had been the APOSTATE OF SORROW, but he would do penance. He would become again what he once had been. He was already starting to resemble the town. Once more he was the brother in silence and in melancholy of this sorrowful Bruges, his *soror dolorosa*. Oh, he had been right to come here at the time of his profound grief! Mute analogies! The inter-

penetration of the soul and physical objects. We enter into them, while they penetrate us.

Towns above all have a personality, a spirit of their own, an almost externalised character which corresponds to joy, new love, renunciation, widowhood. Every town is a state of mind, a mood which, after only a short stay, communicates itself, spreads to us in an effluvium which impregnates us, which we absorb with the very air.

When he first came here, Hugues had felt this pale and soothing influence of Bruges and through it had come to resign himself to living on memories alone, to relinquish hope, looking forward to a Good Death . . .

And now, despite the anxieties of the present, his pain diluted a little, in the evening, in the long, still canals, and he tried to become once more a man in the image and likeness of the town.

# XI

The face of the town is the face of a Believer. It is counsels of
faith and renunciation that emanate from it, from the walls of
its almshouses and convents, from its frequent churches kneeling in their surplices of stone. Once more it started to direct
Hugues, to impose its rule. Once more it became a figure, the
one to whom Hugues principally addressed himself, impress-
ing, dissuading, commanding, his mentor from whom he
derived all his reasons for acting.

Now that he was gradually escaping from the face of sex
and lies that was Woman, Hugues was soon won back to this
mystic aspect of the Town. He listened less to the former and,
as he did so, he heard the bells more.

Countless bells, never tiring. As he lapsed into melancholy
again, he had started going out at dusk once more, wandering
aimlessly along the *quais*.

He found the constant ringing painful: bells tolling for
anniversary or requiem masses, for trentals, calling to matins
or vespers, all day long, swinging their unseen black censers,
giving off a kind of smoke of sound.

Oh, the incessant bells of Bruges, the great service for the
dead chanted through the air without respite! How they
expressed a disgust with life, a clear sense of the vanity of all
things, a warning that death was on its way . . .

In the empty streets where, now and then, a lamp gave a
flicker of life, occasional silhouettes would appear, ordinary
women in their long woollen cloaks, cloaks black as the
bronze bells, swinging like them. And, correspondingly, the
bells and the cloaks seemed to be making their way towards
the churches, taking the same route.

94

Hugues felt himself being guided imperceptibly. He followed in their wake. He had been won back to the surrounding fervour. The persuasion of example, the latent urging of objects led him in his turn to the contemplative calm of the old churches.

He found that once more, as when he first came to Bruges, he liked to tarry there in the evening, especially in the aisles of Saint Sauveur with its long marble slabs, its grandiloquent rood-screen from which, sometimes, waves of shimmering music broke . . .

The music was vast, streaming down from the pipes onto the stones. You would have said it was the music which drowned, erased the dusty inscriptions on the grave slabs and the brass plaques that are scattered everywhere round the basilica. You could truly say you were walking in the middle of death there.

There was nothing, neither the gardens of the stained-glass windows, nor the marvellous, ageless pictures – by Pourbus, van Orley, Erasmus Quellin, Crayer, Seghers with his never-fading garlands of tulips – that could sweeten the sepulchral sadness of the place. Scarcely had Hugues registered the colourful splendour of the triptychs and altarpieces, the immortalised dreams of distant painters, than his melancholy deepened as his thoughts were drawn to death at the sight, on the panels, of the donor, hands folded, and his wife, with cornelian eyes, of whom nothing remains but these portraits. Then he would call to mind his dead wife. He refused to think of her living likeness, of that impure Jane whose image he left at the church door; it was with his dead wife that he dreamt of himself kneeling before God, like the pious donors of the past.

During these fits of mysticism, Hugues also liked to go and bury himself in the silence of the little Jerusalem Chapel. It was there above all that the women in their cloaks went, at sunset . . . He went in after them. The aisles were low-ceilinged, a sort of crypt. At the far end of this chapel, erected for the adoration of the Wounds of the Saviour, is a life-size figure of Christ, Christ in the tomb, leaden-coloured under a shroud of fine lace. The women in their cloaks lit small candles, then left with gliding steps. The candles bled a little, in the murky light one would have said they were the stigmata, opening and starting to flow again, to wash away the sins of those who came there.

But of all his pilgrimages round the town, it was above all the Hospital of St John that Hugues loved to visit, where the divine Memling had lived and where he left some naive masterpieces to convey to generations to come the freshness of his dreams when his health started to recover. Hugues also went there in hope of finding a cure, to bathe his feverish retina in the lotion of those white walls. The great Catechism of Calm!

Interior gardens, bordered with boxwood; sickrooms, far off, where people are talking softly. Nuns pass, scarcely disturbing the silence, as the swans on the canals scarcely disturb the water. A smell of damp linen hangs in the air, of headdresses soiled by the rain, of altar cloths that have just been taken out of ancient cupboards.

Finally Hugues came to the sanctuary of art containing the unique pictures, resplendent with the famous Shrine of Saint Ursula, like a small Gothic chapel in gold, narrating, in three panels on either side, the legend of the eleven thousand Virgins, whilst on the enamelled metal of the roof, in medallions as delicate as miniatures, are angel musicians with violins the colour of their hair and harps in the shape of their wings.

Thus the martyrdom is accompanied by painted music. It is infinitely sweet, the death of these Virgins, grouped like a bank of azaleas in the galley tying up at the quay that will be their tomb. The soldiers are on the bank. They have already started the massacre. Ursula and her companions have disembarked and the blood is flowing, but it is such a rosy colour! The wounds are flowers, the blood does not drip, it falls from their breasts like petals being shed.

The Virgins are happy and perfectly calm, contemplating their courage in the soldiers' armour, which shines like mirrors. Even the bow from which death comes seems as sweet to them as the crescent moon.

What the artist tells us with these subtle strokes is that death, for the devout Virgins, is merely a transubstantiation, a trial gladly accepted in return for the promise of imminent bliss. That is why the peace, which is already within them, has spread to the landscape, suffusing it as if it radiated from their souls.

A moment of transition, less butchery than apotheosis already. The drops of blood are beginning to harden into rubies for their eternal diadems and above the drenched earth heaven is opening up, its light visible, seeping down . . .

Angelic understanding of martyrdom! Paradisal vision of a painter whose piety matched his genius!

Hugues was moved. He thought of the faith of these great artists of Flanders who bequeathed us paintings which are truly votive pictures; painting for them was like prayer for other people.

Thus it was that from all these things around – the works of art, the gold and silver plate, the architecture, the houses that looked like cloisters, the gables shaped like mitres, the streets adorned with Madonnas, the wind filled with the sound of bells – an example of piety and austerity streamed towards Hugues, the influence of a Catholicism ingrained in the very air and the stones.

At the same time the piety of his early childhood came back to him and, with it, a nostalgia for lost innocence. He felt some guilt towards God, as he did towards his dead wife. The idea of sin reappeared. Especially since one Sunday evening, when, going by chance into the cathedral for the benediction and the organ, he heard the end of a sermon.

The priest was preaching on death. What other subject is there to choose in the gloomy town where it is so obvious, compelling even, twisting its vine with the black grapes round the pulpit, within reach of the preacher's hand, so that he only has to gather them? What is there to talk about, if not about what is in the atmosphere everywhere? The inevitability of death! And what other thought to develop than that of the need to save your soul, the main concern, the permanent torment of consciences here?

So the priest, expatiating on a Good Death, a death which was only a transition, and on the reunion of souls that had been saved and reside with God, came to speak of the sin which was the danger, the *mortal* sin, the one that turned death into real death, without deliverance, without rejoining loved ones.

Hugues listened, not without a flutter of anxiety, from beside a pillar. The huge church was gloomy, scarcely lit by a few lamps, a few candles. The congregation merged into a dark mass, almost swallowed up by the shadows. He felt he was alone, that the priest was addressing him, speaking to him. By some trick of chance, or of his overheated imagination, it was as if it was his own case that the anonymous words were describing. Yes, he was in a state of sin! It was no good deluding himself about his sinful love affair, justifying it to himself with the likeness. He was mired in the flesh. He was doing something for which the Church had always reserved its severest condemnation: he was living in a kind of concubinage.

If what our religion says is true, if the saved souls of Christians do meet in heaven, then he would never again see her, his Lost Love, his Saint, because he had not desired her exclusively. Death would simply make her absence eternal, consecrate a separation he had believed temporary.

Afterwards he would continue to live, as now, apart from her, and it would be his eternal torment always to remember her in vain.

Hugues left the church, his mind in turmoil. From that day

on the thought of his sin went round and round, worming its way in, deeper and deeper. He longed for deliverance, for absolution. He thought of confessing to calm the storm, the swell that was threatening to engulf his soul. But he would have to repent, to change his way of life and, despite his daily qualms, his self-accusations, he no longer felt he had the strength to leave Jane and return to being alone.

But still the Town, with its Believer's face, reproached him insistently, confronting him with the model of its own chastity, its strict faith . . .

And the bells played their part as he wandered every evening, racked with anguish, suffering because of his love for Jane, his regret for his dead wife, the fear of his sin and possible damnation . . . The bells argued, at first amicably, giving good advice, but soon growing pitiless, berating him – all around, visible, tangible, so to speak, like the crows round the towers – jostling him, getting inside his head, raping and ravishing him to remove his miserable love, to tear out his sin.

# XII

Hugues was suffering. Day by day the dissimilarities were increasing. He could no longer maintain the illusion, even as far as her physical appearance was concerned. Jane's face had acquired a certain hardness and, at the same time, a tiredness, a line under the eyes which seemed to cast a shadow on the unchanged mother of pearl and the jet pupils. She had also started to indulge once more, as at the time when she had been in the theatre, in her fondness for covering her cheeks in a velvety layer of powder, smearing her lips with crimson and pencilling her eyebrows.

Hugues had tried in vain to persuade her not to use this make-up, which was so out of keeping with the chaste and natural face he remembered. Jane – hard, quick-tempered, sarcastic – mocked him. At such times he called back to mind the sweetness of his dead wife, her even temper, the tender nobility of her speech, like petals falling from her lips. Ten years of life together without a quarrel, without a single one of those harsh words that rise from the bottom, like mud, when the soul is disturbed.

Now the differences between the two woman were becoming clearer with every day. No! His dead wife had not been like that! The obviousness of it distressed him, cancelling out what had been the excuse for the affair. Now he was beginning to see how tawdry it was and was overcome with a feeling of embarrassment, almost shame. He no longer dared think of the woman he had mourned so deeply and towards whom he was starting to feel guilty.

He hardly went into the rooms where the souvenirs of her

were preserved any more, disturbed by the look from her portraits, a look, one would have said, of reproach. Her locks still rested in their glass casket, almost abandoned, accumulating a grey film of dust.

More than ever he felt impotent, rudderless. Going out, coming back, going out again, driven, so to speak, from his home to Jane's, drawn by her face when he was apart from it and overcome with regret, remorse, self-contempt when he was together with her.

His domestic arrangements were in disarray as well: no punctuality, no organisation. He would give orders, then change them, cancel his meals. Barbe no longer knew how to plan her work, what food to get in. Troubled, sad, she prayed for her master, knowing what was the reason . . .

Often notes arrived, bills demanding significant sums of money for purchases made by that woman. Barbe, who took them in her master's absence, was stunned: a stream of outfits, trinkets, ruinously expensive jewellery, all sorts of items she obtained on credit, using and abusing her lover's name in the shops of the town where she was ceaselessly buying things, with a prodigality that mocked expense.

Hugues gave way to her every whim, but she was not in the least grateful. She went out more and more, sometimes disappearing for a whole day, for the evening as well, putting off rendezvous she had made with Hugues, writing him hurried notes.

She claimed now to have met people, to have made some women friends. Should she live all by herself like this for ever? Another time she announced that her sister was ill, a sister she had never told him about who lived in Lille. She had to go and see her. She was away for several days. When she came back the same game, the irregular way of life, continued – going out, staying out, shuttling to and fro, in all directions – an ebb and flow in which Hugues's life was suspended.

Eventually he became suspicious. He spied on her, went

prowling round her house in the evening, a nocturnal ghost in the sleeping town. He spent long hours observing from cover, waiting breathlessly, ringing the bell and hearing its quivering chime die away in the silent corridors, standing in the full blast of the wind until late into the night watching a lighted window, the blind a screen on which a shadow play appeared, a silhouette he every second expected to see doubled.

It was no longer his dead wife he was pursuing, it was Jane, whose charms had gradually cast their spell over him and which he was fearful of losing. It was no longer just her face his vision evoked, it was her flesh, entire, burning, on the other side of the night, whilst he could only see her shadow floating over the folds of the curtains . . . Yes, he must love her for herself, since he was jealous, jealous and suffering to the point of tears when he kept watch on her, at night, lashed by the chimes of midnight, the fine rain, incessant in these northern climes where the clouds fray in unceasing drizzle.

And he stayed there, walking back and forth, in a confined space, as if in an exercise yard, talking out loud in the indistinct speech of a sleepwalker, despite the attentions of the rain – slush, mud, cloudy skies, late winter, all the desolate sadness of things . . .

He would have liked to know, be certain, see . . . Oh, the agony! What must she be like, this woman, to make him suffer in this way, while at height of his distress, the other woman – his angel, his dead wife – seemed to rise up in the dark, looking at him with the pitying eyes of the moon.

Hugues was not taken in any more. He had caught Jane lying, put together clues. And he was soon fully informed when, according to the custom of provincial towns, the letters started to pour in, the anonymous cards full of insults, sarcastic remarks, details of her unfaithfulness, the dissolute ways he already suspected. So this was the result of the casual liaison into which what at the beginning had seemed quite plausible reasons had led him. As for the woman – he would break

with her, that was that! But how could he make up for his failure towards himself, for the mockery he had made of his mourning, for the laughing stock his sacred rite, his cult of his dead wife and his sincere despair had become?

Hugues was in torment. Jane was finished for him. It was as if his dead wife were dying a second time. Oh, what had he not had to endure from this capricious, unfaithful woman!

He went to see her one last time, to relieve himself, by saying farewell, of the weight of sorrow accumulated in his soul because of her.

Not out of anger, but with infinite sadness, he told her that he knew everything, and as she responded indignantly, turning on him with an air of defiance – 'What? What are you saying?' – he showed her the denunciations, the shameful letters.

'You're stupid enough to believe anonymous letters?' And she started to laugh, a cruel laugh, exposing white teeth made for tearing prey apart.

'It was your own tricks that had already opened my eyes,' Hugues remarked.

Jane, suddenly furious, paced up and down, slamming doors, the skirts of her negligée fluttering behind her. 'So what?!' she exclaimed. 'What if it is true?'

Then, after a pause: 'Anyway, I'm fed up with living here. I'm leaving.'

Hugues had been watching her while she was speaking. In the bright light of the lamp he saw once more her clear face, her black pupils, her golden hair, dyed, false, as false as her heart and her love! No, that was no longer the face of his dead wife. But the woman quivering in her negligée, breast heaving, was the woman he had embraced, and when he heard her declare, 'I'm leaving!' his heart sank to the depths, plunging him back into infinite darkness . . .

In this solemn moment he felt that, after the illusions of the mirage, of the likeness, he had also come to love her with his senses, a belated passion, a melancholy October inflamed by a fortuity of late-flowering roses.

All his thoughts were swirling round and round in his head. Just one thing he was certain of: he was suffering, he was in pain, and his suffering would cease if Jane stopped threatening to leave. He still desired her, just the way she was. Inside, he was ashamed of his weakness, but he could no longer live without her . . . Anyway, who knows? The world is such a vile place? She had not even attempted to refute the accusations.

He was suddenly seized with a feeling of profound anguish at the end of this dream, which he sensed was in its death throes (love affairs when they break up are like a death in miniature: they too have their partings without farewell). But at that moment it was not the separation from Jane, nor the breaking of the reflecting mirror that distressed him the most. Above all he felt a horror at the idea of being left alone, face to face with this town, without anyone between him and it any more. Of course he had chosen it, this Bruges beyond remedy with its grey melancholy. But the weight of the shadow of its towers was too heavy. Jane had somehow made him feel their shadow was held up above his soul; now he would have to endure its whole weight. He was going to be alone, prey to the bells. Even more alone, as if widowed for a second time. The town, too, would seem more dead to him.

Hugues, in panic, flew towards Jane, grasped her hand and begged, 'Stay, stay. I was mad . . .' in a plaintive voice, damp with tears, as if he had been crying inside.

Returning home along the *quais* that evening he felt uneasy, apprehensive of some danger or other. He was assailed by funereal thoughts, haunted by memories of his dead wife. She seemed to have returned, hovering in the distance, wrapped in a shroud in the mist. More than ever Hugues considered himself at fault towards her. Suddenly the wind got up. The poplars beside the water moaned. The swans in the canal he was walking along were troubled by the turbulence, the beautiful swans that have been there for centuries, that had come down from a coat of arms, according to the legend, expiatory swans the town was condemned to maintain in perpetuity for having unjustly put to death a lord who bore them in his armorial bearings.

The swans, usually so white and calm, were alarmed, emotional, fevered, tearing the watered silk of the canal around one of them that was flapping its wings and, leaning on them, was lifting itself up out of the water, like a sick man thrashing about when he wants to get out of bed.

The bird seemed to be in pain, it was crying out at intervals. Then, as it soared up into the air, its cry was softened by distance. It was a wounded voice, almost human, a real song, modulating.

Hugues looked on, listened, disturbed by the mysterious scene. He remembered the popular belief. Yes, the swan was singing! So it was going to die, or at least sensed death in the air.

Hugues shivered. Was the ill omen intended for him? He had been only too well prepared for these dark forebodings by the cruel scene with Jane, her threat to leave. What else was going to finish in him? The superstitious night was wearing black, but for whom? If he was to be widowed again, what would be his loss?

# XIII

Jane turned the warning to her advantage. With the intuition of an adventuress, she realised what power she had over Hugues, who was so infatuated with her, she could do with him as she liked.

A few words and she had reassured him completely, won him back, had come out untarnished in his eyes, returned to her pedestal. She had calculated that at his age, weighed down for so long by grief, ill as he was, so changed even over the last few months, Hugues would not live for long. He was considered rich; he was a foreigner and alone, without acquaintances in this town. What a fool she would have been to let that inheritance slip through her fingers when it would be so easy for her to secure it.

Jane moderated her behaviour a little, going out less frequently, providing plausible explanations, being more prudent in the risks she took.

She had conceived the desire of going at some time to Hugues's house, that immense, ancient mansion on the Quai du Rosaire with its air of opulence, its impenetrable lace curtains, like frost tattooed on the windows, allowing no hint of what was inside.

Jane would have very much liked to gain admittance to his home, to estimate, from its luxury, his probable wealth, to assess his furnishings, his silverware, his jewels, everything she coveted, to make a mental inventory, on the basis of which she would come to her decision.

But Hugues had never agreed to let her visit him there.

Jane was all tenderness. It was like a new beginning for

them, a new dawn, pink and warm. It so happened there was a favourable opportunity. It was May and the following Monday was the centuries-old Procession of the Holy Blood, in which the Reliquary containing a drop of blood from the Wound made by the lance was taken round the town.

The procession would go along the Quai du Rosaire, passing outside Hugues's windows. Jane had never seen the famous procession and expressed curiosity about it. It would not pass her house, which was too far out; how could she see it when, so it was said, the streets that day were crowded with people who had come from all over Flanders.

'How about it? I'll come to your house . . . we can dine together . . .'

Hugues objected that the neighbours, the servants would talk.

'I'll come very early, when everyone's still asleep.'

He was still concerned at the thought of Barbe, so prudish and pious, who would see her as an emissary of the devil.

But Jane was insistent. 'Right? That's agreed then?'

She had that cajoling voice, the voice of beginnings, the voice of temptation that all women have at certain moments, a voice like a crystal glass ringing in an ever-widening, swirling nimbus of sound in which the man is caught up, yields and lets himself go.

# XIV

That Monday Barbe had got up with the dawn, even earlier than usual, because she would only have part of the morning to deck out the house before the procession passed.

She went to early mass, at half past five, then started her preparations as soon as she got back. The silver candlesticks were taken out of the cupboards, little silver-gilt vases, burners for incense. Barbe rubbed and polished each object until the metal shone like a mirror. She also took out fine cloths to cover the small tables she placed at each window to make nice little household altars for the month of Mary, with candles round a crucifix, a statue of the Virgin . . .

She also had to think about decorating the outside, because it is a day when neighbours vie with each other to show their pious zeal. Already fixed to the front of the house, according to custom, were the fir trees with branches of green bronze the peasants sell from door to door, forming, along the streets, a double hedgerow of trees.

On the balcony Barbe arranged draperies in the papal colours, white cloth in an array of chaste folds. She bustled round the house, unctuous, respectful in her handling of the decorations, which were used every year and which, for her, had the sanctity of liturgical objects, as if they had been con-secrated by the hands of a priest, by chrism, by ineradicable holy water. She felt as if she were in a sacristy.

All that was left was to fill the baskets with herbs and flowers, a shifting mosaic, a scattered carpet with which each servant will colour the street outside her house the moment the procession passes. Barbe worked hurriedly, slightly intoxi-

cated by the scent of the mallows, the large lilies, the mar-
guerites, the sage, the aromatic rosemary, the reeds she was
slicing into short strips. Her hand, plunging into the baskets as
they filled, was freshened by this massacre of petals, cotton-
wool clouds of freshness, down from dead wings.

Through the open window came the crescendo of parish
bells as they started swinging one after the other.

The weather was grey, one of those indecisive May days
when, despite the clouds, the sky carries a hint of joy. And
because of this fineness of the air, in which the bells could be
discerned making their way, a gladness spread from it to her.
The ancient, tired-out bells, the hobbling ancestors, the bells
of the convents, of the old towers, the stay-at-homes who
look after their health and keep quiet all year, but set off and
join the Procession of the Holy Blood, they all seemed to have
covered their gowns of worn brass with joyous white surplices, linen fluted in fanlike folds. Barbe listened to the peals,
the big bell of the cathedral that was only heard on the great
feast days, slow and black, like a crozier hitting the silence . . .
and also the little bells of all the spires close by – an exuberance, a jubilation of silvery gowns which seemed to be lining
up in a procession in the sky as well . . .

Barbe's devout soul was elated. It felt, on that morning, as if
there was a fervour in the air, as if the sky were shedding
raptures with the bells ringing their hearts out, as if one could
hear invisible wings, angels flying past.

And all this seemed to be directed at her soul, her soul
where she felt the presence of Jesus, where the host, which she
had taken at the dawn mass, shone forth, still whole, in its full
orb, at the centre of which she saw a face.

The old servant, thinking of the loving-kindness of Jesus,
who truly dwelt within her, crossed herself and started to pray
again, recalling the Host, the taste of it on her tongue.

However, her master had rung for her, it was time for his
breakfast. He took advantage of her appearance to tell her he

was expecting someone for lunch and that accordingly she was to make arrangements.

Barbe was astounded. It seemed strange to her, he had never had a visitor before. Suddenly an awful thought crossed her mind. What if the thing she feared, the thing she had, somewhat reassured, put out of her mind, were to happen? She reflected . . . yes, it must be that woman, the one Sister Rosalie had spoken of, who was going to come.

Barbe felt the blood freeze in her veins. In that case her decision was made, her duty plain. Her confessor had clearly forbidden her to open the door to this creature, serve her at table, be at her beck and call – to be party to sin. And on such a day! The day when the blood of Christ was going to pass outside the house! And she herself, who had taken communion that morning! . . . No, it was impossible. She would have to leave on the spot.

She wanted to know, and with that petty tyranny servants quickly assume in bachelor or widower households in these quiet provincial backwaters, she asked, in insinuating tones, 'Who has monsieur invited to dinner?'

Hugues replied that it was a little presumptuous of her to question him like that, she would know when the person arrived.

But Barbe, obsessed by her idea, which was coming to seem more and more likely, seized with fear and real panic, decided to risk all so as not to be caught unawares. She asked again, 'It wouldn't perhaps be a lady monsieur is expecting?'

'Barbe!' Hugues exclaimed with an astonished and somewhat stern look.

But, without flinching, she went on, 'It's because I have to know in advance. Because if it's a lady monsieur is expecting, then I must inform monsieur that I will not be able to serve his lunch.'

Hugues was stunned. Was he dreaming? Had she gone mad?

116

But Barbe repeated emphatically that she was going to leave, she couldn't do it; she'd already been warned; her confessor had ordered her to. She had no intention of disobeying, flagrantly, of putting herself in a state of mortal sin – perhaps to die suddenly and end up in hell.

At first Hugues could not understand at all. Gradually he managed to disentangle the confused web: the probable gossip, his affair noised abroad. So Barbe knew as well? And was threatening to leave because Jane was going to come? She must be very much despised for this humble servant – attached to him for years by habit, interest, the thousand threads which each day weaves between two people who live side by side – for her to prefer to make a complete break and leave him, rather than serve the woman for one day.

This abrupt annoyance, which so unexpectedly spoilt the pleasant prospect of the day ahead, left Hugues drained, dumbfounded, powerless to act. He simply said, 'In that case, Barbe, you may leave at once.'

The old servant looked at him and suddenly, seized with pity like the good, if simple soul she was, realising how he was suffering, murmured, in that crooning voice nature has given us to lull children to sleep, with a shake of the head, 'Oh, Jesus. Poor monsieur! And for a woman like that, a bad woman . . . who is unfaithful to you . . .'

For a moment, forgetting the distance between them, she had been maternal, ennobled by divine pity, in a cry that bubbled up like a soothing, perhaps healing spring . . .

But Hugues told her to be silent, irritated, humiliated by this interference, the audacity of talking to him about Jane – and in such terms! It was he who was dismissing her, and without reprieve. She could come and collect her things the next day, but for now she had to leave, to leave at once.

Her master's exasperation removed any remaining scruples Barbe might have had about leaving him so abruptly. She put on her fine black cape with its hood, pleased with herself, with having sacrificed herself to duty, to Jesus, who dwelt within her . . .

Calmly, with no show of emotion, she left the house where she had lived for five years. But before setting off, she scattered outside it the contents of the baskets, which she had emptied into her apron, so that the street beneath the feet of the procession would not be without petals in that one place alone.

# XV

What a bad beginning to the day! Joyful projects must be a challenge to fate: prepared too far in advance, they give it time to switch the eggs in the nest so that it is woes we hatch out.

Hearing the door close as Barbe left, Hugues had a painful feeling. Another annoyance, even greater solitude, since the old woman had gradually come to be part of his life. And all because of Jane, that cruel, capricious woman. Oh, the suffering he had gone through because of her!

He would be happy now if she did not come. He was sad, unsettled, irritated. He thought of his dead wife . . . How could he have come to believe the lie of that resemblance, so quickly marred? And what must she be thinking, in the afterlife of the tomb, of the arrival of another woman in the home that was still so full of her, sitting in the armchairs she had sat in, superimposing, as she passed the mirrors in which the faces of the dead persist, her features over his dead wife's.

The bell rang. Hugues was forced to go and open the door himself. It was Jane, late, red from having walked quickly. She swept in, imperious, taking in at a single glance the wide corridor, the rooms with their doors open. The sound of distant bands could already be heard approaching. The procession would not be long arriving.

Hugues had lit the candles Barbe had set out on the window-ledges and little tables.

He went up to his room on the first floor with Jane. The windows were closed. Jane went over and opened one.

'No, no,' said Hugues.

'Why not?'

He pointed out that she could not show herself, could not flaunt her presence in his house. Especially to watch a religious procession. Provincial towns were prudish. There would be an outcry.

Jane took off her hat at the mirror and smoothed a little powder over her face with the puff from a small ivory box she was never without. Then she went back to the window, her hair uncovered, its light, coppery tints catching the eye.

The people crowding the street stared, curious about this woman who was not like the others, with her showy clothes and hair.

Hugues lost patience. With a sudden burst of energy he closed the window violently.

Jane took umbrage, refused to watch and sat down on the sofa, expressionless, hard.

The procession was singing. The shimmering ripples of the hymns widened, announcing its approach. Hugues, aching with unhappiness, had turned away from Jane. He rested his burning forehead against the window-pane, the freshness of water in which to soak away all his anguish.

The first altar boys were passing, shaven-headed singers chanting, holding candles.

Through the window Hugues could see the procession clearly, with the various figures standing out like robes painted on the background of religious images made of lace.

The congregation walked past, carrying pedestals with statues, Sacred Hearts, holding banners of hardened gold, like stained-glass windows; then came the groups of the innocent, the orchard of white robes, the archipelago of muslin with incense wafting up in little clouds of blue, a conclave of child virgins around a Paschal Lamb, as white as they and made of curled snow.

Hugues turned round for a moment to Jane, who was still ensconced in the sofa, sulking, looking as if she were thinking spiteful thoughts.

122

The deeper tones of the serpents and ophicleides rose up, sweeping the frail, intermittent garland of the sopranos' voices along with them.

Then, framed in the window, the Knights of the Holy Land appeared before Hugues, the crusaders in cloth of gold and armour, the princesses from the history of Bruges, all the men and women associated with the name of Thierry of Alsace, who brought the Holy Blood back from Jerusalem. Playing these roles were young men and women from the most noble families of Flanders, wearing ancient materials, rare lace, centuries-old family jewels. It was as if, brought to life by some miracle, the saints had been made flesh, the warriors, the donors of the pictures by van Eyck and Memling, perpetuated down there, in the museums.

Hugues was scarcely taking it in, distressed by Jane's pique, feeling infinitely sad, even sadder in the hymns that caused him almost physical pain. He tried to appease her.

At the first word her hackles rose and she turned her eyes on him, bristling, as if her hands were full of things that were going to wound him even more.

Hugues withdrew back into himself, silent, upset, casting his soul, so to speak, onto the waves of music swirling through the streets, so that they would carry it far away from him.

Then it was the ecclesiastics stepping past, monks from all the orders, Dominicans, Redemptorists, Franciscans, Carmelites; following them came the seminarists in pleated surplices, singing from antiphonaries, and the clergy of all the parishes, clothed in red like altarboys: curates, priests, canons, in chasubles, embroidered dalmatics, resplendent like gardens of precious stones.

Now the jingling of censers could be heard. Wreathes of blue smoke rolled closer and all the little bells united in a more resonant hail of sound that made the air vibrate.

The bishop appeared, wearing his mitre, under a canopy, carrying the shrine – a small cathedral in gold, surmounted by a cupola where, dreaming amid thousands of cameos, diamonds, emeralds, amethysts, enamels, topazes, fine pearls, lies the single ruby of the Holy Blood.

Hugues, overcome by a mystical feeling, by the fervour on all the faces, by the faith of this immense crowd gathered in the streets, under his windows, farther off, everywhere, right to the edge of this town in prayer, bowed down too when he saw, as the reliquary approached, all the people fall to their knees, bend beneath the blast of the hymns.

Hugues had almost forgotten the reality of the situation, the presence of Jane, the new scene that had placed more barriers of ice between them. Jane, seeing him so moved, sniggered.

He pretended not to hear, stifling the spurts of hatred he was beginning to feel for this woman.

Disdainful, glacial, she put her hat on again, apparently preparing to leave. Hugues could not find the strength to break the heavy silence which had fallen on the room now the procession had passed. The street had quickly emptied, was already quiet, with the intensified sadness of joy departed.

Without a word, she went down the stairs. Then, when she reached the ground floor, as if she had changed her mind or felt a sudden curiosity, she looked into the downstairs rooms, whose doors had been left open. At first she stood on the threshold, then she took a few steps, going a little further into the two vast rooms with a communicating door between them, as if reproved by their severe appearance. Rooms, too, have a physiognomy, a face. Between them and us there is sympathy or antipathy at first sight. Jane felt she received a frosty reception, didn't belong, was at odds with the mirrors, hostile to the old furniture, whose unchanging attitudes her presence threatened to disturb.

She looked round, inquisitive . . . She saw portraits scattered about, on the walls, on the little tables, the pastel portrait, the photographs of Hugues's dead wife.

'Oh, you've got pictures of women here?' And she laughed, an unpleasant little laugh.

She went over to the fireplace. 'Well, well, well, here's one that looks like me . . .' and she picked up one of the portraits.

Hugues, who was watching her, increasingly uneasy at seeing her going round these rooms, suddenly felt a sharp pain at her thoughtlessly cruel playfulness, at her excruciating banter, which tainted the sanctity of his dead wife.

'Put that down!' he said, his voice suddenly imperious.

Jane burst into laughter, uncomprehending.

Hugues went up to her and took the portrait out of her hands, shocked at the sight of those profane fingers on his relics. He only handled them with a tremor, like liturgical objects, as a priest would the monstrance and the chalices. His sorrow had become a religion. And at that moment the candles, which had burnt on the window-ledges for the procession and not yet gone out, lit up the rooms like chapels.

Jane, sarcastic, perversely amused at Hugues's irritation and secretly wanting to make more fun of him, had gone into the other room, touching everything, knocking over the trinkets, crumpling the fabrics. Suddenly she came to a halt with a resounding laugh.

She had seen the precious glass casket on the piano and, to continue her show of defiance, lifted the lid, took out, with an expression of amused astonishment, the long tresses, unfurling them, holding them up and shaking them.

Hugues had gone deathly pale. That was a profanation. He had a feeling of sacrilege. For years he had not dared touch this object, which was dead, since it came from a dead person. And all this worship of the relic, all those tears stippling the glass every day, only for it to end up as a plaything for a woman who mocked it . . . Oh, she had made him suffer long enough, too long! All his rancour, all the suffering he had swallowed, soaked up, every second of every hour, for months on end, the suspicions, the betrayals, the watching at her

window, in the rain, it suddenly all came back to him . . .
Throw her out, that's what he would do.

But as he darted towards her, Jane, as if in play, took refuge
behind a table, defying him, holding the plait away from
him, bringing it up to her face, to her lips, like a charmed
snake, winding it round her neck, a feather boa from a golden
bird . . .

'Give it back,' Hugues cried, 'give it back.'

Jane ran, this way then that, round and round the table.

Hugues, in the frenzy of the chase, with her laughter, her
sarcastic remarks, lost his head. He caught her. She still had the
plait round her neck, resisting, refusing to give it up, angry and
insulting him now because the grip of his fingers was hurting.

'Will you?'

'No!' she said, still laughing, though it was a nervous laugh
as his grasp tightened.

Hugues saw red. A flame was buzzing in his ears, the blood
stinging his eyes, his head filled with dizziness, he felt a sudden
frenzy, a tingling at the tips of his fingers, a desire to clutch
something, to squeeze it, to crush flowers, his hands like a vice,
with all its strength – he had grabbed the hair, which Jane
still had wrapped round her neck, he wanted it back! Grim,
distraught, he pulled at the long plait round her neck, tighten-
ing it. Taut, it was as stiff as a rope.

Jane was not laughing any longer. She gave a little cry, a
sigh, like the breath from a bubble expiring on the surface of
the water. She fell to the floor, strangled.

*

She was dead, dead from not having comprehended the
Mystery, and that there was something that must not be
touched on pain of committing sacrilege. She had laid her
hand on the avenging tresses, those tresses which, from the
outset – for those who are pure of soul and in communion
with the Mystery – let it be understood that the moment they

were profaned they would themselves become *the instrument of death*.

Thus in fact the whole house had perished: Barbe had gone, Jane was lying dead, his dead wife was even more dead . . .

As for Hugues, he was looking without understanding, without knowing any more . . .

The two women had fused into one. So alike in life, even more alike in death, which had given them the same pallor, he could no longer distinguish one from the other, the single face of his love. Jane's body was the ghost of the other dead woman, visible there for him alone.

Hugues's mind had regressed, now he could only remember things from a long time ago, the early days of his life as a widower, to which he believed he had been taken back. Very calmly he had gone to sit down in an armchair.

The windows were still open . . .

Into the silence came a sound of bells, all the bells at once, which had started to ring again for the return of the procession to the Chapel of the Holy Blood. The fine display was over, everything that had been in it, had been sung – a mere semblance of life, resurrected for one morning. The streets were empty again. The town was going to be solitary once more.

And Hugues kept repeating, 'Dead . . . dead . . . dead town . . . Bruges-la-Morte . . .' mechanically, in an expressionless voice, trying to match – 'Dead . . . dead . . . dead town . . . Bruges-la-Morte . . .' – the cadences of the last bells, weary and slow, little, worn-out old bells which seemed to be shedding petals – was it on the town? was it on a grave? – from flowers of iron.

*Translated by Mike Mitchell*

# PART 2

# INTRODUCTION

Melancholy, solitude, morbidity, neuropathic tendencies and the unresolved longing for an imagined past are all classic hallmarks of the symbolist mind-set. Together they are the leitmotif which runs through both *Bruges-la-Morte* and the accompanying essay, *The Death Throes of Towns*. It is no coincidence that both have the word death in the title. For Rodenbach this was an overwhelming preoccupation, whether as reality in the background to his own life or as an aesthetic represented by the landscape of Bruges. Although in the novel Rodenbach is concerned with the trials and obsessions of the protagonist Viane, whose fate embodies the ebb and flow of human failure and resilience, it is, as Rodenbach reminds us, the dying town itself which is the principal character of the novel. Amidst the turmoil of Hugues and Jane's relationship, we are served a series of *récits* or accounts on diverse aspects of the town's character and atmosphere. Despite the unfolding drama of the novel, Rodenbach just can't help sidling off into the Béguinage or one of the Bruges churches for a crafty monologue. The hallucinated image of death sending its black vine twining around the pulpit and up to the outstretched preacher's hand during the sermon, or the sublime lyrical interpretation of the legend of the shrine of St Ursula by Memling are memorable examples of this literary compulsion.

The reader will soon note that there are striking similarities between such excerpts in the novel and those in the *The Death Throes of Towns* text. It is almost as if Rodenbach lifted these straight out of the essay and grafted them onto the novel.

In some cases they are almost word for word. *Agonie de Villes* to give the French title, appeared some years before the appearance of *Bruges-la-Morte*, in 1889. It was originally published as one of a series of articles, but did not appear in book form until 1924, long after the author's death, when thanks to the efforts of Rodenbach's daughter and his faithful biographer Pierre Maes, it formed the opening piece in a series of literary essays to which they gave the name 'Evocations'.

Rodenbach places Bruges, 'the dethroned Queen,' at the head of a clutch of other 'dead towns' such as Ypres, Furnes and Courtrai, those 'melancholic widows of medieval Communes', which between them made up an area of Flanders Rodenbach referred to as a 'cemetery'. Belgian symbolism is rooted in place to a greater degree than its French counterpart and these low-lying canal towns were in effect appropriated by the symbolists as ideal landscapes from which to evoke the sensations of drawn-out decline and aesthetic decay their psychology demanded. The influence of Schopenhauer's ascetism on that psychology cannot be underestimated. His radical ideas on seclusion and mysticism were crucial to symbolist thought in the closing decades of the nineteenth century. Both here in the essay and in the novel such pre-occupations are clearly evident.

Rodenbach soon established his reputation as the leading protagonist of what became loosely known as 'dead-city prose'. He was able to express himself with great effect over a variety of mediums: poetry, drama, the novel and in this case the essay. Other Belgian writers like Camille Lemonnier and Franz Hellens also took up the theme which characterises *The Death Throes of Towns*. Hellens *En Ville Morte,* published in 1906, concentrated on Bruges' sister town Ghent to express a vision of existential affliction and unrelieved devastation. Hellens' funereal preoccupation gives the impression that the town is literally decomposing, the very walls assailed by disease and pestilence, mirroring the terminally sick condition of mankind. Hellens seeks to go beyond the death throes evoked by Rodenbach but risks getting lost in his own labyrinth of histrionic metaphor and relish for putrefaction.

Rodenbach on the other hand, in *The Death Throes of Towns,* balances his role as inspirational travel guide and historical interpreter of Bruges with the task of symbolist poet seeking to give the impression of a once healthy medieval town replete with pageantry and self confidence now slipping in and out of consciousness, a permanent invalid. Rodenbach deliberately confuses the town with the sick who lie in the silent alcoves of the St Jean hospice overlooking the canal. Like them, Bruges wakes from a coma to find herself bandaged and dressed but no longer aware of her identity. He identifies the condition of the town with human sickness. 'How moving it is in this centuries-old consumption, in which the town stricken with death spits out one by one her stones – like lungs . . .' Alongside such extravagantly morbid metaphors, he talks with great passion of the splendour of churches and palaces, the quiet passage of the pious inhabitants, the Procession of the Holy Blood, the untrammelled haven of the Béguinage and the guarded mystery of the canals. Furthermore, he treats each with an intimacy and reverence gained from assiduous observation. A rare and revealing photograph shows him perched on a fold-up chair relaxing in the meadow of the Béguinage with notebook in hand, simply watching and waiting. But always there is a darkness hovering, a sense of engulfment, some nameless tragedy poised to smother everything. Take his determination to draw out the underlying nature of that most imposing Bruges landmark. '. . . and beyond the harsh belfry, the colour of wine lees, of rust, of blood and a waning sun, unadorned, lacking any cheerful sculpture, tragic and bellicose, leaving for the heavens, as if to war, with the arrows of its pinnacles and the mighty shield of its dial.'

Rodenbach once declared that his aim was to be for Bruges

what Turner was for Venice. He wished to paint the true soul of the town, to capture both the reality of Bruges in his own time and a mythical town which resonated with the past. Rodenbach was only too aware of the wealth of art which Bruges had guarded over the long centuries of decline and even in his own time, despite the first stirrings of modernization, the town was still an artistic haven. It was hardly surprising that his endeavours to reveal the aesthetic and artistic side of the town appealed to Parisian literary tastes and cemented his reputation in the French capital. Rodenbach's visionary compulsion to personalise the town and focus on the hidden life behind objects seemed for many to draw out the underlying romantic soul of Bruges and encouraged a revival of literary travellers to make their pilgrimage north. The most notable of these was Rilke, who, naturally sympathetic to Rodenbach's vision, even stayed at Furnes, another of the dead towns, to acclimatize himself before tackling the main prize, Bruges.

Little escapes his gaze, but it is in his evocation of the canals themselves that Rodenbach excels himself. Time and again he returns to them both in the novel through Hugues' interminable wandering, here in the essay and also in his other novels and poetry. More than any other element of Bruges, it is the canals which have bewitched Rodenbach since early childhood. Their serenity, innate mystery and undisturbed form serve to arouse a plethora of analogies and exert a profound melancholic significance. The degeneration of the canalside 'furniture' is another rich source from which to extract those raw materials required to cultivate the desired 'state of the soul'. Here as in the novel, Rodenbach follows the line of the canal, alighting on those time-worn and atrophied objects clinging to the water's edge, gathering them in for the sensations they might arouse within the solitary who harbours a secret intimacy with their lonely fate. '. . . and above the lifeless waters, overhanging balconies, wooden balustrades, railings leading to untended gardens, mysterious doorways, a whole range of muddled, crooked things crouched at the water's edge, as if begging, beneath rags of tattered foliage and frayed ivy.'

The subtle collage effect of sight and sound, colours, nuances of light and shade, or weather and season which one notes in the novel is prefigured in the essay. It is the coalescence of these autonomous properties that sustains the atmosphere of melancholy. Everything is draining into something else and nothing is acting alone. This feeling is enhanced by his close observance of water, the interminable streaming and dripping, the seeping from gutters and roofs into the stillness of the canal. Equally so in his depiction of the purity of reflection or stillness and their inevitable violation. Through the poet's relentless probing the town has almost become an amorphous being. As Rodenbach himself affirms, 'all this overwhelms the onlooker in one profound mortuary impression which little by little the town reveals to us . . .'

As in the novel, Rodenbach pays great attention to the Béguinage, or that 'mystic enclosure' whose rustic meadow recalls the paintings of Van Eyck, lacking only the paschal lamb, a symbolic isle of calm and pureness of purpose which seems resigned to remain permanently under siege from the dying town. This closing section of the essay leads to a remarkable passage on the nature of silence. The convent seems to represent for Rodenbach the ultimate seclusion demanded in order to access a more sustaining inner self, an ideal of purity far removed from the corrosive effects of the crowd and the deceptions of the external world. But there is some ambiguity here. For the poet the atmosphere of overwhelming extinction he experiences in the Béguinage is also an endorsement of the fate which awaits the solitary. Like Hugues Viane in the novel who is surprised to find himself, despite the decrepitude of his soul, the only survivor of the all encompassing death, Rodenbach offers a chink of light which quickly fades with the suggestion of suicide; 'one gradually submits to the creeping counsel of the stones . . .' As if to confirm this, he follows with a reference to the drowning of Shakespeare's Ophelia, where the waters, instead of waiting inertly for their victim, instead take on a state of being and 'come to meet her grief.' This image is repeated almost word for word in the novel. Rodenbach rounds off his essay with a brief but powerful sequence which might be said to prefigure Rilke's reflections along similar lines, 'the silence seems like something living, real, something despotic which is there, alone, as if in a kingdom chosen for its exile, which seeks, commands, and displays hostility to anything which disturbs it. Unconsciously you submit to its silent pain . . .' But silence works to exaggerate solitude and acts as a restraint on reality. It acts as a balm to the agonized spirit but also represents a mysterious force whose true nature remains ambiguous. The silence of the canals is a 'lesson' to Hugues Viane. Any noise that erupts threatens to injure this state of muted melancholy resignation. In the novel, even the sound of musical instruments is unbearable, and voices themselves have the capacity to actually physically injure one's being and reopen wounds. Ironically only the bells of Bruges are permitted to break this silence, 'like a drizzle of dark flowers, like the dust of cold ashes from these urns which sway gently from the distant towers . . .'

*Will Stone*

# THE DEATH THROES OF TOWNS

## An essay by Georges Rodenbach

Towns are rather like women: they have their time of youth-fulness and blooming, then comes decline and the cracks appearing each day along the walls, painfully increase the lines of their ageing. How many who not so long ago were hand-some and wealthy towns, suffer an abandonment at their life's end; poor ancestors who grow stiff with an air of fallen grace, preserving at the most a few monuments: coats of arms in stone, armorial bearings which alone attest to their ancient and authentic nobility. Most turned to mysticism, trans-formed into nuns, who, in the evening, tell the iron rosary of their bells!

Above all in Flanders, Flemish Flanders, in this provincial silence so near and yet so distant, there are such towns fallen into destitution or oblivion: Ypres, Furnes, Courtrai, Aude-narde, those melancholic widows of medieval Communes; but among such downfalls of history and that most lamentable distress that is a town in its death throes, it is Bruges, the dethroned queen, who today is dying the most taciturn and moving of deaths. For Bruges, now forgotten, impoverished, all alone with her empty palaces, was truly a queen in Europe in another age, queen to a sumptuous court of legend, beside the waves, a queen that Venice, envious beyond the far horizon, bowed down to like a less fortunate sister.

So how has this splendour of gold and rich fabrics given way to decline, for a town which now shivers in the bareness of its stones?

Here is how the drama unfolds. Once the town was linked to the sea by the Zwijn, which via Damme sent a channel of deep water as far as Bruges, a royal river, where 1700 ships sent by Philip Augustus against the Flemish and English could easily manoeuvre. Thus ships from all corners of the globe could reach as far as Bruges and moor along her quays. One day in 1475, however, the North Sea suddenly retreated and as a result the Zwijn dried up, without them being able to dredge it clear or re-establish a flow of water; and henceforth, Bruges, now at some distance from that mighty breast of the ocean which had nourished her children, began to bleed dry and for four long centuries lay in the shadow of death.

How moving she is in this centuries-old consumption, in which the town stricken with death spits out one by one her stones – as if from her lungs – and especially moving on this autumnal November morning, beneath a sky whose pallor is in perfect accord with her own! Here and there, a scattering of golden palaces, polychrome, set like jewels, vast caskets of stone that the dispossessed queen has kept. And beyond, the harsh belfry, the colour of wine lees, of rust, of blood and of a waning sun, unadorned, lacking any cheerful sculpture, tragic and bellicose, setting off for the heavens, as if to war, with the arrows of its pinnacles and the mighty shield of its dial. While the immense tower leaves the town at its feet and casts a vast indifferent shadow over her, the towns-women, like servants of her death throes, and with an air of commiseration, go about their business in the remoteness of the streets, their steps muffled by the moss and grass between the cobblestones. They are entombed in a great cloak with stiff folds whose raised hood covers their entire head. This is the local dress, a bell of black cloth swinging to and fro in melancholy motion, and there in the distance you feel you can hear their steps dying away like a death-knell.

Today there is a certain sweetness in walking around the lethargic town, through dreams and memories, down streets

never straight, ever capricious, supplying at each step of one's stroll, a surprise or something unforeseen. Oh! The ancient and exquisite facades with carved bouquets fading away, cartouches in which satyrs disintegrate in the weathering of the stone, the heads of women whose lips the dust and rain robbed of their bloom.

Ornaments everywhere, a curiosity, a symbol, an emblem, coats of arms or signs that time has dulled as if with the ashes of centuries!

Everywhere flights of steps with balustrades, everywhere gables which rise in regular steps like stairways, scaled by glances invited by a bird of iron at the very top, or some inconsolable weather vane. On the walls, cryptic signs in numerical form which attest to their authentic antiquity; bas reliefs, still enduring though half-eaten away; bricks in a crimson of dried blood, scored by age-old wounds, and shields emblazoned with a lion or half-moon swaying on rusting rails at the door of old hostelries. And in windows the panes a mournful bluish green, set in their diamond of lead, so nothing happens outside the interior life of these dwellings, as if abandoned and dead!

Here the muteness of sounds matches that of the colours as all the facades fade in nuances of yellowed pallor, washed-out greens, antiquated pinks that sing softly the silent melody of faded hues. Who knows what obsession of candles and incense pursues one through this maze of calm streets. At each crossroads Madonnas stand in cases of glass, clothed in velvet and lace, crowned with silver, honoured with flowers and votive offerings. And the roadside crucifixes, the chapels, the shrines where there are relics to be kissed, candles to be lit upon iron frames with their black spikes, and finally the great churches with their immense towers encircled by funereal crows: Saint-Sauveur and Notre-Dame, where one scarcely takes in the density of decoration, so sumptuous, the marbles, the rich wood carving, the florescence of stained glass, the

145

accumulation of works of art, amongst which the Virgin of Michelangelo shines out.

All this coalesces in one profound mortuary impression which little by little the town reveals to us and which is sustained even here in the sombre cathedral where reside those moving tombs of Charles the Bold, lying on his back, hands folded in prayer, feet upon a lion, symbolising strength, and of Mary of Burgundy, in a gown of marble, her feet resting on a heraldic greyhound, symbol of fidelity. And so many other tombs: all the slabs are memorial stones, with skulls, names chipped away, inscriptions already eaten into as if by lips of stone. Here death itself is expunged by death!

But on certain days, all springs into sudden and unaccustomed life. As if to the call of an invisible trumpet that the angels had raised to their lips, all the Virgins and the Sacred Hearts descend from their pedestals; the banners quiver as if they were gowns that had been put on. And now the door is opening: it's the feast of the Holy Blood and in the first warm spell of May the Procession leaves here and moves off through the revivified town: altar boys in crimson robes: little girls in their hundreds, all in white, in snowy muslin, shedding petals from baskets, leading the Paschal Lamb decked with ribbons; the Knights of the Holy Land, the Crusaders in armour and cloth of gold; the princesses of Bruges history mounted on caparisoned horses, dressed in the most sumptuous and authentic costumes.

For in these processions or historical corteges it is the young men and women from the most noble families in Flanders who take on the prominent roles, using old fabrics, lace from the past and the family jewels. And here come the monks of all orders chanting to the accompaniment of the brass: Dominicans, Franciscans, Oratorians, Carmelites; then the clergy of the seminary, the priests, vicars, canons in dalmatics, in chasubles embroidered with gold and silver,

resplendent as gardens of jewellery. Finally, in the cloud of incense, bells of all sizes and voices, psalms, the Bishop appears, mitre on head, beneath a canopy, carrying the precious crystal where that single ruby of the Holy Blood bleeds for all eternity.

And you might think it all a dream, this lavish spectacle in the dreary streets and that for just one day, by some miracle, the characters from the sacred canvases of Van Eyck and Memling who slumber in the museums, had come back to life, become flesh and blood.

It is a moment of illusion in her centuries-old abandonment. Hugo said: 'You disturb the grass, and the dead are happy'. But the disturbance quickly passes and today as I lead you there, the peace of a cemetery reigns in those deserted districts and along the taciturn quais.

These quais of Bruges, how in my pensive youth I followed, confessed, loved them: with secret places I alone knew about and consoled, houses whose dead windows watched me!

And in the prison of those quais of stone, the stagnant water of the canals where no more ships or small craft pass, where nothing is reflected other than the stillness of the gables, whose crow-steps traced on the water seem like stairways of crepe leading to the very bottom. And above the lifeless waters, overhanging balconies, wooden balustrades, railings round untended gardens, mysterious doorways, a succession of muddled, crooked things crouched at the water's edge, as if begging, beneath tattered rags of foliage and ivy.

And, as if to wash the corpse of the lifeless waters, there is the eternal weeping, the streaming and dripping of the gutters, the drains and sporadic springs, the overflow from the roofs, the seepage from the tunnels of the bridges, like a great euphony of sobbing and inexhaustible tears.

Oh! The invisible mourners, the tears of things in which

one truly senses an almost human sorrow! Only the great solitary swans, the legendary swans of these canals, have enlivened this mourning over centuries, divine birds of snow and enchantment, coming here from who knows where, descended from some armorial bearings, if one believes the legend whereby the ancient town was obliged to maintain the presence of the swans on the canals in perpetuity to atone for the unjust condemnation of a lord who bore the swans on his coat of arms.

But the memory of blood no longer haunts those sublime expiatory birds, for they sail along so peacefully in their whiteness. And the poet, like Lohengrin, feels drawn by them towards the outlying districts, also in their death throes, and to the beauty spots of the Minnewater, a name with exquisite resonances, the 'lake of love', as it is literally known, but better still perhaps: the waters where one loves! And here, before this gentle lake strewn with water lilies, where night releases its rosary of stars, the dream is truly aroused, the scattered silences interweave their meshes into a net of melancholy in which little by little all words fold in their wings. And far off the mighty quiver of towers, turrets, spires bristling the horizon, and the towers – God alone knows what shadows they are casting now over our hearts!

Amongst the ramparts, a few melancholy windmills whose sails wearily turn. In the distance they seem to be slowly grinding down a patch of pale sky.

And now right before us, huddled up for warmth beneath a cloak of greenery, with a long enclosing wall like a cemetery of souls, stretches the grey and confused mass of the Béguinage.

The Béguinages! These singular and unique convents linger on in Flanders, in the sorrowfulness of dead towns, not only in Bruges and Ghent, but in those more lowly and decayed: Courtrai, Termonde, Malines, those poor little towns whose bells are like defiant quavering voices.

The Béguinage, a town apart within the town, a mystic enclosure which remains a place of undisturbed prayer.

At its centre a lush grassy lawn: rich and luxuriant like a meadow by Jan Van Eyck. All around lanes bordered on each side by walls as white as the cloths for the communion table. In these walls the doors, painted green, are elaborately decorated with coloured images or ironwork, with the name of each convent, sweet names, sounding sweet. The 'House of Angels', the 'House of Flowers', the 'House for the Consolation of the Poor'; or even the 'House of St Béga', sister of Pépin, who was, they say, the founder of the order.

All these separate little convents house some twenty nuns, living communally, subject to the same discipline and obedience, and all answering to the Reverend Mother.

They also all attend the same services, so it is not uninteresting to go to the church at the hour of Mass and the Benediction. For according to the rule, when entering they place over their heads a voluminous starched veil which falls to the ground in stiff creases; then they go and kneel side by side and it seems as if, above all in Ghent, where the Béguinage comprises some twelve hundred nuns, a glacier of white pointed cones is coming to rest beneath the flight of the hymns.

What distinguishes the order is that their time here is probationary, unbound by any religious vow, and they are at liberty to leave of their own free will from those liberal convents, to return to the world, to enter into marriage. But such a thing is rare. They live there in such peace, so removed from life, passive, unconscious, beneath the linen halo of their cornets, their sole dream to deck the altar with meticulous fingers for the holy month of Mary and the novenas.

After the services, their hours are taken up with needlework, but as if these virgin fingers could only handle something white, they embroider and stitch linen or make lace. In the workroom with its pale blue walls, they are seated in a circle and their nimble fingers play with the bobbins on a great frame where the threads tangle around copper pins in a spread of white blooms!

In the Béguinage of Bruges, the surrounding decay has also decimated the holy population cloistered there. Half of the smaller convents are vacant, and the few nuns who remain hardly seem alive in the enclosure replete with absence. Vaguely discerned behind fastened windows, one would take them rather for the shades of former nuns come to bring to those still chambers, to the forsaken Madonna, some fresh flowers from paradise.

Outside, in the sleepy peacefulness of the lanes, not a sound is heard, not even an echo, only a breath of wind in the great trees whose stirring leaves sigh like a spring whose lament has all but dried up. How distant the town! The dead town! And it is for her funeral that a bell in the distance chimes! Now others are ringing out, but so vague, so ponderous, like a rain of dark flowers, like the dust of cold ashes from these urns which sway gently from the distant towers.

And peace, disturbed for a moment by this agreeable exhilaration of space, spreads until it floods even the breathing of things. You walk with soft steps, as in a house where a corpse rests. You don't even dare speak.

For at this moment the silence seems like something living, real, something despotic which is there, alone, as if in a kingdom chosen for its exile, a will, commanding, displaying hostility towards anything which disturbs it. Unconsciously, invincibly, you suffer its mute pain and if by chance some passer-by approaches and makes a noise, you have the sense of something abnormal occurring, something shocking and sacrilegious. Only a few béguines with light rustling steps can reasonably move about there, in this dead atmosphere, for they seem less to walk than to glide, they are other swans, the sisters of the white swans of the long canals. And in the vast mystic

enclosure one is surprised to be the only survivor of the death all around; one gradually submits to the creeping counsel of the stones, and I imagine that a soul, bleeding from some recent, cruel sorrow, that had walked amidst this silence, would leave that place accepting the order of things – not to live any longer – and, beside the neighbouring lake, sense what those gravediggers of Shakespeare said of Ophelia: it is not she who goes to the waters, but the water which comes to meet her grief.

*Translated by Will Stone*

# RODENBACH
# REMEMBERED?

A note on the failure to erect a memorial

In vain will the visitor to Bruges search for a significant memorial to the most famous poet associated with it. Unfortunately the town authorities have signally failed to erect a substantial statue or sculpture to the poet largely because the fiercely patriotic Flemish are to this day dismissive of, or at least irked by the French-dominated culture of the period in which the book was written, at a time when Flemish nationalism had barely asserted itself. All past efforts to erect a monument, even by important literary figures, have been quashed by the town authorities. The puritanical townspeople of Bruges a century ago were aghast that their city should have the reputation for being a mausoleum and that the melancholia induced by its decaying landscape was the primary incentive for curious travellers. They set about changing that image and suppressing the idea that Bruges was a moss-covered tomb, deep in coma, sustained on the drip of its illustrious past. The prevailing idea was that writers like Rodenbach in adopting the French language had somehow sold their Flemish souls in seeking to satisfy snobbishly refined Parisian literary tastes whilst discarding the 'real people' of Flanders, who were left behind to grinding poverty in the wake of these extravagant, supercilious dandies. The reality was of course much more complex, for it was nigh impossible at that time for writers of the calibre of Rodenbach or his Ghent schoolmate Verhaeren to avoid the cultural powerhouse of Paris for long. Their very vocations depended on the associations and relationships that the French capital provided. And to be fair, in his prose and poetry Rodenbach eagerly shows his love for, and writerly fidelity to the landscape of Flanders. The notion of those who left for Paris being traitors has persisted in some sense to this day and can be easily gleaned in random conversation on the streets of Bruges. However, the considerable foreign attention and cultural investment Rodenbach has brought to the city, not to mention the reverential attitude of his writings concerning it, should surely merit him a far more substantial memorial and dignified stature in the public's imagination. But no such reference or civic memorial exists even to this day for a poet who in terms of notoriety and importance to Bruges, is equal to the relationship between let us say Kafka and Prague. Thankfully there are unforeseen dividends, as yet there are no umbrellas, tee-shirts and tea towels emblazoned with the face of Georges Rodenbach for sale along the quai du Rosaire. To find a proper memorial to the poet one must travel to the 'Grand Béguinage' of Ghent where the sculpture by Georges Minne, originally destined for Bruges, was finally erected in 1903 after much wrangling. A committee had been formed, headed by Verhaeren, to organize the building of a memorial for Rodenbach. Such was Rodenbach's profile as a poet in Paris, Rodin himself had even offered to provide a sculpture which could stand near the entrance to the Béguinage in Bruges, but the enthusiastic French-speakers immediately came up against fierce Flemish opposition from the Catholic authorities of Bruges, ardently supported by local poet Guido Gezelle. Eventually the committee was obliged to seek an alternative location for the memorial. And of course the irony is that today Gezelle conveniently fills the role of poetic son to Bruges, with prominent statues, streets named after him and even his own museum. One is more likely to come across Rodenbach on a menu, as one of the more popular local beers happens to bear that name. Recently a modest and discreetly placed bronze plaque was defiantly erected by some heroic admirer on the side of a house at the Van Eyck Plein, but really this is wholly insufficient. This shameful situation is one which the Flemish authorities seem steadfastly unprepared to tackle. After all, as long as the tourists keep coming, why should they bother?

*Will Stone*

# A Note on the Photographs

As the prefatory note to the novel indicates, the original 1892 edition of *Bruges-la-Morte* included thirty-five half-tone reproductions of Bruges street scenes and views of the town's principal landmarks. These photographs were hardly ever produced in their entirety in subsequent editions. Only the Garnier-Flammarion edition reproduces all of them. Because of the relative brevity of the novel it meant that originally there were photographs every few pages. It was decided for this edition that, in keeping with the original images would indeed be used, but that it might be more interesting and stimulate debate to include modern photographs of Bruges. The original photographs are not dissimilar from those sepia images now sold in souvenir shops all over Bruges and with these antique landscapes in mind, I duly set out to photograph the town. Despite the passing of time it was clear that a number of those views to be found in the original images were being reproduced or at least ones which curiously evoked them. Readers who are familiar with the original photographs may be surprised to note how effectively Bruges has resisted the erosion of its architectural soul and unique psychology, if only in photographic terms. We have interspersed the photographs within the text of the novel and have also included a selection in the essay 'The Death Throes of Towns'. As far as possible I have tried to place the image where it has most relevance to the text.

# Acknowledgements

I would like to thank the following individuals and organisations whose support for the *Bruges-la-Morte* project meant that my task was made that much more enjoyable and fulfilling. Firstly, the 'Collège européen des traducteurs littéraires de Seneffe' in Belgium who awarded me several residencies to work on Rodenbach and Verhaeren. Thanks also go to the 'Bureau du livre français à l'étranger' in Paris who awarded me a translation bursary as part of the Burgess Programme and to Arts Council East here in the UK, from whom I received a further grant to carry out essential research in Bruges and Brussels. I should like to extend my thanks to Paul Edwards for his crucial work on the photographs of *Bruges-la-Morte*, to Anthony Rudolf in London and Professor Clive Scott at the University of East Anglia for their unflagging support and lastly Anette and Marc Van de Wiele, whose wonderful bookshop behind the cathedral in Bruges supplied me with such a wealth of relevant information, and for their infectious enthusiasm, warmth and Hospitality.

*Will Stone*

# Dedalus European Classics 1984–2021

The Dedalus European Classics series exists to rescue neglected authors and publish authors who have yet to be translated into English, as we widen what constitutes a classic to include the bizarre and the fantastic from the late 19th century to the middle of the 20th century and work from the small linguistic areas of Europe.

Many of the authors we have published in this series were not at the time felt to be classic authors but we have in most cases made them so. We also like to produce a body of work so a reader can judge an oeuvre and not just a book. We have established or re-established the reputation in English of J.-K. Huysmans, Giovanni Verga, Octave Mirbeau, Gustav Meyrink, Johann Grimmelshausen and Eça de Queiroz by having new translations made of their work and for the first time having a whole oeuvre available in English.

In our thirty-fifth year we are trying to get as many titles as possible back into print so our readers can enjoy nearly all the titles in the Dedalus European Classics list in a print edition. Some titles will remain as ebooks only and some will not be available in the foreseeable future. We have put an estimated publication date for titles which will shortly be reprinted or printed for the first time.

# Dedalus European Classics by author:

1  The Little Angel  *Andreyev*
2  The Red Laugh  *Andreyev*
3  As Train Pass By (Katinka)  *Bang*
4  Ida Brandt  *Bang*
5  Séraphita  *Balzac*
6  The Quest of the Absolute  *Balzac*
7  Senso (and other stories)  *Boito*
8  The Fiery Angel  *Bruisov*
9  Dark Vales  *Casellas*
10  The Devil in Love  *Cazotte*
11  Sappho  *Daudet*
12  Les Diaboliques  *D'Aurevilly*
13  The Angels of Perversity (new ed 2021)  *de Gourmont*
14  The English Family  *Dinis*
15  Undine  *Fouqué*
16  Toomas Nipernaadi  *Gailit*
17  Misericordia  *Galdos*
18  Spirite  *Gautier*
19  The Dark Domain  *Grabinski*
20  The German Refugees  *Goethe*
21  The Continuation of Simplicissimus  *Grimmelshausen*
22  The Life of Courage  *Grimmelshausen*
23  Simplicissimus  *Grimmelshausen*
24  Tearaway  *Grimmelshausen*
25  Against Nature  *Huysmans*
26  The Cathedral  *Huysmans*
27  Drifting  *Huysmans*

28 En Route *Huysmans*

29 Là-Bas *Huysmans*

30 Marthe *Huysmans*

31 Modern Art *Huysmans*

32 The Oblate *Huysmans*

33 Parisian Sketches *Huysmans*

34 Stranded (En Rade) *Huysmans*

35 The Vatard Sisters *Huysmans*

36 Marie Grubbe *Jacobsen*

37 Waves *Keyserling*

38 The Fables of Ivan Krylov *Krylov*

39 The Other Side *Kubin*

40 The Road to Darkness *Leppin*

41 The Mystery of the Yellow Room *Leroux*

42 The Perfume of the Lady in Black *Leroux*

43 Monsieur de Phocas (new ed 2021) *Lorrain*

44 The Woman and the Puppet *Loüys*

45 The Angel of the West Window *Meyrink*

46 The Dedalus Meyrink Reader *Meyrink*

47 The Golem *Meyrink*

48 The Opal (and other stories) (new ed 2021) *Meyrink*

49 Walpurgisnacht *Meyrink*

50 The White Dominican (new ed 2021) *Meyrink*

51 Abbé Jules *Mirbeau*

52 The Diary of a Chambermaid *Mirbeau*

53 Le Calvaire *Mirbeau*

54 Sebastien Roch *Mirbeau*

55 Torture Garden *Mirbeau*

56 Smarra & Trilby *Nodier*

57 The Late Mattia Pascal *Pirandello*

58 The Notebooks of Serafino Gubbio *Pirandello*

59 Tales from the Saragossa Manuscript *Potocki*

60 Chasing the Dream *Pougy*

61 A Woman's Affair *Pougy*

62 Manon Lescaut *Prevost*

63 Eugene Onegin *Pushkin*

64 Alves & Co *Queiroz*

65 The City and the Mountains *Queiroz*

66 Cousin Bazilio *Queiroz*

67 The Crime of Father Amaro *Queiroz*

68 The Illustrious House of Ramires *Queiroz*

69 The Maias *Queiroz*

70 The Mandarin (and other stories) *Queiroz*

71 The Mystery of the Sintra Road *Queiroz*

72 The Relic *Queiroz*

73 The Tragedy of the Street of Flowers *Queiroz*

74 Monsieur Venus (kindle ed only) *Rachilde*

75 The Bells of Bruges *Rodenbach*

76 Bruges-la-Morte *Rodenbach*

77 Celestina *Rojas*

78 The Great Shadow (new ed 2021) *Sà-Carneiro*

79 Lucio's Confession *Sà-Carneiro*

80 The Class *Ungar*

81 The Maimed (new ed 2021) *Ungar*

82 I Malavoglia *Verga*

83 Mastro Don Gesualdo *Verga*

84 Short Sicilian Novels (new ed 2021) *Verga*

85 Sparrow, Temptation & Cavalleria Rusticana *Verga*

86 Autumn & Winter Sonatas *Valle-Inclan*

87 Spring & Summer Sonatas *Valle-Inclan*

88 L'Innocente (The Victim) (ebook only) *D'Annunzio*

## The Bells of Bruges – Georges Rodenbach

'There are few novels that quickly astound. This is one of them. Flawlessly translated, this elegiac romance, first published in 1897, is a masterpiece of sublime power. Joris Borluut, the town bell ringer, marries the tempestuous Barbara but the match turns sour and an affair with her sister ensues. Acutely rendered as this thread is, it is always subservient to the real story, that of Bruges itself.'      Martin Tierney in *The Herald*

'Mike Mitchell's translation of *The Bells of Bruges* opens with one of the most arresting scenes I read in the shortlist. A crowd gathers to hear bell-ringers compete for the office of town carilloneur: "Here, in the meditative land of Flanders, among the damp mists so antagonistic to the brilliance of fire, the carillon takes their place. It is a display of fireworks that one hears: flare, rockets, showers, a thousand sparks of sound which colour the air for visionary eyes alerted by hearing." The novel is a story of love and obsession, of two beautiful sisters and a man who marries the 'wrong' sister, of an artist in sound whose dedication to his office has something terrible in it. But the dominant character is the city of Bruges, which comes to possess the reader's imagination as it has possessed Rodenbach's and then Mitchell's. This is a beguiling translation, which captures a Lawrentian intensity of sensuous experience.'

Helen Dunmore, novelist and chair of the
*Oxford Weidenfeld Translation Prize* judges.

'The novel appeared in 1897, five years after Rodenbach's hugely successful *Bruges-la-Morte*. Where *Bruges-la-Morte* was a short, poetic psycho-drama of death and eroticism, *The Bells of Bruges* (given here in Mike Mitchell's nuanced but unfussy translation) is a long and crowded novel that touches on everything from nineteenth-century obsessions with progress and decline, to tourism and town planning... There are intertwined plots as there are in *Bruges-la-morte*. Borluut is caught between two women, the dark, fiery Barbara and the ethereal, pale Godelieve. Between them they represent, on the one hand, the earthy, Latin side of Belgian culture (Barbara is more than once referred to as a Spanish beauty, an allusion to Flander's history as a Spanish colony), and its Nordic, mystical side, Rodenbach's obsessive symmetry is such that he provides Borluut with bells that also represent this: a small, clear, tuneful bell and a large, dark bell inlaid with obscene orgiastic images, a 'bronze dress' up which he loses himself. Sex and death are never far away in Rodenbach, either from each other or from the surface of the story. As the novel's extraordinary climax shows, *The Bells of Bruges*, is no exception.'

Patrick McGuinness in *The Times Literary Supplement*

**£9.99   978 1 903517 54 3   244p   B. Format**

## Hans Cadzand's Vocation (and other stories) –
## Georges Rodenbach

'Georges Rodenbach, the Belgian Symbolist, died in 1898 but his writing is so modern it might have been written in this century. He eschews the heavy descriptions of most 19th century oeuvres for a lightness of touch that allows the reader to dance over the pages. *Hans Cadzand's Vocation* is a novella taking up most of the book, followed by a few very short stories. Illustrating the motto 'Beware What You Wish For', it tells the story of Hans, whose father dies when he is a baby, leaving a mother dependent on him for her emotional needs. He becomes an altar boy and while his mother dreads him falling in love, she ignores his religious devotion until he declares he wants to take holy orders. She tries to match him with the pretty daughter of a friend and, when that fails, hires a sexy maid to seduce him. His failure to resist temptation makes him give up his dream but his desolation infects his mother as he still lives with her. Every morning they display their sadness to the world as they make their way to and from church. Rodenbach's other stories show why he left Bruges to live in Paris. The Belgian city is a place of sadness and death so overwhelming that a Parisian artist and his mistress, who leave stale marriages to live together in Bruges, find the lifeless atmosphere extinguishes their passion and leaves him unable to paint. Priests and religion dominate conventional Bruges, while Paris inspires laughter and art.

Scarlet MccGuire in *Tribune*

**£7.99   978 1 903517 86 4   168p   B. Format**

### Lucio's Confession – Mário de Sá-Carneiro

'Written in 1913 this is a thoroughly decadent story of an unusual *menage-à-trois* which ends in a killing. It's filled with poets and artists and those special problems that sensitive people have ('Do you hear that music? It's like a symbol of my life: a wonderful melody murdered by a terrible unworthy performer.') The last word on this magnificent period piece – bejewelled and opiated and splendidly over the top – belongs to one of its characters: "It seems more like the vision of some brilliant onanist than reality".'

Phil Baker in *The Sunday Times*

'Febrile, intense and innovative.'

Nicholas Lezard in *The Guardian*

'An enigmatic love triangle riddled with madness and jealousy, set in *fin-de-siecle* Paris and Lisbon, and its translation reopens a rich vein of fantasy.' Christopher Fowler in *Time Out*

'The story of an enigmatic and unusual *menage-à-trois*, with a strong homoerotic subtext, set in a world of fantasy and madness.' Keith Richmond in *Tribune*

**£8.99   ISBN   978 1 873982 80 8   121p   B. Format**